HIDDEN WISHES

DJINN EVERLASTING BOOK THREE

LISA MANIFOLD

 Created with Vellum

FOREWORD

If you haven't read the prequel novella, Heart of the Djinn, I recommend that you do! It's the story of how Dhameer ended up meeting Tibby, and then Xavier and Bryant. You can get your copy here! Just click on the image, and I'll send you the file!

Or, if you can't click, go to www.lisamanifold.com/djinnnews

SEE HOW IT ALL BEGAN...
READ DHAMEER'S STORY IN HEART OF THE DJINN

CLICK HERE TO DOWNLOAD

1

I was so nervous, I could feel my palms sweating. Everything was sweating. I resisted the urge to rub my hands against my legs.

I took a deep breath. Looked into the eyes of my future, hopefully. "I love you. The past four years have been the best of my life. I want to spend the rest of it with you. Will you marry me?"

Then I held my breath.

"Yes!"

I threw open my arms and welcomed my heart into them.

---

*B*irthdays were supposed to be fun. That had been my plan.

Had been. Now, mine would be fun in comparison to, say, a head-on collision. I looked at the man across from me. How had this gone so wrong?

Ten minutes ago, we were laughing and crying

together. I'd asked him to marry me, and he'd said yes. He was surprised, which surprised me.

Until he'd asked about my dinner plans this evening. He knew that I had a standing dinner with my family on my birthday. But Graham wouldn't be going with me—he knew this. He knew all this. My family didn't know the truth of my life.

We'd had this conversation before. I knew I was a coward for having it yet again. But I couldn't do anything different. Not right now.

"I don't give a rat's ass how they are. That won't work anymore, Bryant. This is on you." He said as he put his hands on his hips, waiting.

I couldn't hear his words over the roaring in my ears. This was the point I'd been trying to avoid for four years— my whole life, if I were honest. Which I wasn't, and that was the problem. There was no more room for avoidance.

"I can't," I said.

"Well, that's pretty clear." He looked at me with a hard look and turned and left the room.

"Wait! What about what we just decided?" I followed him.

We spoke, but whatever we said fell from my head. All I could see was him walking out, and the noise of him going down the stairs.

He'd left me.

I'd asked him to marry me, and he said yes. Then he said no, and he left.

What else was there to say?

I had to think about this. I turned and went up the stairs to bed.

There was nothing else I could do. Not right now.

I lifted the corner of my mouth to try to keep the smile on my face. I'd practiced this in the mirror, so that I didn't completely piss off my family and start a fight where there were no winners.

But as usual, my birthday celebration seemed to be more what they thought it should be rather than what I wanted. I would have preferred to have everyone over to the townhouse, and cook, and eat and drink and talk. That was it. That was my idea of how to celebrate.

Instead, we were out at a restaurant with fine linen and china. None of the kids were there. Dad was going on about the firm, Casey and Matt nodding and joining in when they had to—it also seemed that they were as uninterested as I was—in some weird attempt to make me miss what I'd never wanted.

My mom tried to keep the peace. Granddad made witty quips, generally stirring the pot.

Another year down.

Another year where I felt that no matter what, it wasn't going to be enough of my family. What pissed me off was that later tonight, I'd go home and have wine, and unlike the past four years, Graham wouldn't be there to share it with me, and laugh over the absurdity of my family.

Tonight, however, I'd be feeling sorry for myself rather thankful that I'd escaped the planned life.

Because I was never going to go along with what Dad had drilled into my head for years. Although, God knows I'd tried. All through high school, I tried. Took all the right classes. Associated with the "right" people. My brothers were athletes (I was okay) and dated the cheerleaders. Like, all of them.

So I asked out the junior varsity cheerleaders, to moderate success. While none of us ever spoke of it, they didn't seem any more interested in getting handsy with me than I did with them. I think all the girls who agreed to go out with me were more impressed with who my brothers were than who I was.

In college, I used the excuse of law. I had to get good grades to get into the pre-law program. I was determined to go to Georgetown, and that wasn't an easy task, even for me, with my last name. It worked, and once Tibby and I became good friends, I would take her as a date to places where one was required.

It worked.

My mom wondered if we were dating, my brothers asked how I'd scored her, and my dad said, if you marry her, get a prenup.

Granddad just laughed. Ever since he'd met Tibby when we'd asked him to bankroll our partnership, he loved her. Said she was going to be a kick-ass attorney, and he wanted her to owe him one.

We both did. One of the proudest moments of my life was five years after Tibby and I set up shop. We were able to repay my grandfather's loan to us in full. I think I actually saw tears in the old man's eyes.

My dad was less sentimental. "It's time to settle down, now. You're solvent, you don't owe Dad anymore, and you need to think about your future."

I made a non-committal noise and edged away. I didn't even have Tibby anymore as she'd married Seth over the summer.

"Now that Tibby seems to have moved on," my mother added helpfully.

"Mom, I'm nothing but happy for her."

"Better he's not with her, Marg," my dad said. "What happens if they split? Then they would have to divide a marriage and a practice."

"Thanks for looking out for me, Dad."

"Well, someone has to."

I rolled my eyes, kissed my mom, and left. Family dinners were less and less enjoyable.

And no, no one had to look out for me. I looked out for myself just fine. Shit like this was getting old.

My brothers did it too, like I was still the baby of the family, never quite measuring up. The fact that I had my own practice, and they were still working for partnerships in theirs, and Tibby and I were well-off—that didn't seem to mean anything.

To my family, I was still Baby Bryant. Add on Single Bryant, and my mom had a constant tone of lament.

But I couldn't tell them the truth.

I'd never brought home a girl to my mother. If I got married, it would be to someone just like me—tall, blond instead of brunette, career-minded, not really interested in kids, and male.

The family, of course, had no idea. Which made the events of earlier today even worse.

I sighed. I could go over and over things until my head imploded, and it wouldn't change what had happened, or that I'd have to try to pick up the pieces of my life.

Calling Tibby would be great because she knew the truth. To talk to someone who knew, who got it—it was a luxury. But she was married, and it wasn't appropriate for me to call at all hours of the night like we used to

No matter what she said.

I'd have to get through this on my own.

*T*he next morning, I got to work early, before anyone else. I dived right into the things that needed to be taken care of, happy to have something to distract myself.

But by midmorning, I shoved the papers on my desk off to the side. I loved my work even though international shipping wasn't an exciting branch of the law. Working with our clients to navigate the laws of various countries in relation to the US was fascinating, and resembled a big, tangled ball of yarn. You had to be patient to work your way through it.

I wasn't in the mood today.

"Hey, can you—" Tibby came in with a sheaf of papers in her hand. "What is it?"

She was always sensitive to my moods. It's one of the reasons I loved working with her. She knew me, knew the real me. Knew pretty much everything about me and loved me as I was.

Even when I'd taken her now-husband out clubbing to a gay bar. She'd come and picked the three of us—her friend, now mine, I guess, Xavier was with us as well—in the middle of DC in the ass early hours of the morning when we were drunk as lords without complaint. The only thing she said was that no one was to throw up in her car.

Other than friendly ribbing that was the end of it. Tibby was more family than anyone I'd been born into a relationship with.

"I don't know. Family dinner was fairly annoying. They seem to think I fucked it up with you somehow, which is why you rebounded with a client's grandkid."

Tibby burst out laughing. "When do you ever fuck up, Bryant? You're one of the most meticulous people I know!"

"Well, not according to my family."

She dropped into a chair in front of my desk. "Why are they more on your nerves lately? I've never heard you complain about them like you have been."

I shrugged. I knew I was bitching more, but I couldn't help it. "Because now I'm supposed to do the right thing, settle down, get married, and contribute to the tribe." I grimaced. "You know. The world needs more Higgs."

"You'd be a great dad," Tibby didn't miss a beat. "Look at all the shit you saved my stupid ass from."

"That's true, but it was always such a softball with you," I grinned at her, thinking about the biggest almost oops on her part. That was when I told her the truth about me. We were interning for the same firm, and at the annual Christmas party. We'd gotten to be friends in class, but I wasn't close to her. No one was, really.

I could still see her now, at that Christmas party years ago, that she should have been networking at, but instead she was drinking too much. She and one of the partners, Gerry the asshole, had wandered down the hallway to the bathrooms together. Anyone not drunk could see the intention happening there. Mrs. Goodman, or Mrs. Gerry-the-asshole, saw it too. Her lips tightened, and after a moment, she squared her shoulders, and leaned over to speak to one of the other partner's wives.

Oh, shit. It was about to go down. I didn't want Tibby to get the wrath of the scorned wife because I could tell that Mrs. Goodman wasn't the type to blame her husband.

While she was debating, I set my drink down on the nearest table, and practically ran down the hallway.

Stupid as hell, they were right out in the open, sucking face. Being drunk was no good for anyone. I came closer and touched Tibby on the shoulder.

"Tib! There you are. Come here and hurry your ass up!"

At that, the partner did look up. *"Mind your own business, buddy"*, he slurred, and then turned his attention back to Tibby.

I moved closer, and instead of kissing the asshole, Tibby looked at me. When Gerry leaned in for more, she pushed him away with a little shove.

"What the hell..." Gerry-the-asshole muttered.

"What is it, Bryant?" Tibby asked.

"His wife is headed this way. If she catches you, it won't be him she's mad at. C'mon, Tib. Don't be stupid. Come with me and save your ass."

"Piss off, you little punk," said Gerry.

I ignored him. "Tib, you know I'm here for you. Not like this guy," I said with a look of disgust, glaring at Gerry.

It seemed like everyone was waiting to hear what Tibby would say. If this went wrong, my internship would be toast. But I'd seen what Mrs. Goodman did to secretaries who pissed her off. Someone touches her man? Tibby would lose hair, at the very least. I didn't want that to happen to her.

As one of her study partners, I had plans for our friendship. Which meant she couldn't screw this up with Gerry-the-asshole.

2

"*You're right, Bryant. So not worth it,*" *Tibby said, giving Gerry another shove.* "*Lead on. Get me the hell outta here.*"

"*I don't think we can. C'mere and do your best.*" *I hissed. I could hear the wife coming closer.*

"*Wha—*" *Tibby began, but I yanked her toward me. I pulled into the other side of the hall in an alcove leading to the bathroom and laid a kiss on her. None too soon, either. The angry footsteps were getting closer. I tried to concentrate on making the kiss convincing, but I found I was thrown off a bit by the fact that Tibby was shaking. From fear, or nerves, I didn't know. Stay calm, I thought. Don't blow it now, Tib!*

"*What in the hell?*" *Said Gerry.*

"*Gerald!*" *Said an angry voice. The click-clacking of heels on tile stopped.*

"*What? What, honey? I'm right here,*" *Gerry said, sounding much more alert.*

"*What are you doing? I've been looking for you everywhere!*" *Oh, yeah. She was pissed. Rightfully so.*

"*I had to go to the bathroom!*" *said Gerry.*

God, he sounded pathetic.

"Well, what are you doing standing in the hallway?" She asked.

"They're blocking the door!" he said defensively, and I could tell he was blaming us for his whatever.

"Excuse me!" said the woman, the noise from her heels coming closer to where I stood with Tibby.

"Hmmm, sorry?" I said, breaking away from Tibby, sounding dazed. "Whatdidja say?" I hoped she wasn't too alert to the fact that I wasn't drunk like her husband and Tibby. To me, I sounded ridiculous, slurring my words like this, but if she bought it, that's all that mattered.

"You are blocking the door to the restroom! Please take this... this whatever it is... somewhere else," she said.

"What? Oh!" I said, as though I'd just realized where we were, who she was. "Mrs. Goodman! I'm sorry! We just wanted a little privacy, didn't realize anyone else was here. Sorry about that. C'mon, Tib, let's go home." I looked down at Tibby with an adoring smile.

She giggled and said, "All right, honey. Probably a good idea." Tibby hugged me close and then smiled up at Mrs. Goodman. As though she wasn't just kissing Gerry-the-asshole moments ago.

I didn't think I imagined that Mrs. Goodman looked slightly disappointed. What, she wanted to catch them?

Oh. I bet she did. Then she'd have an excuse to be angry, all without needing to deal with her husband and his actions. Convenient. I looked at her again. What a horrid bitch this woman was.

Then I remembered I wanted to get us out of here unscathed, so I relaxed and smiled at the old dragon. "Again, sorry about blocking the way."

"Yeah, really sorry," Tibby said with a bright smile. "We'll get out of your way now."

We headed down the hallway, arms around one another like any other couple, and we hadn't gotten far when we heard her start whisper-yelling at her husband.

He totally deserved it.

"Let's get our stuff and get the hell out of here," I said quietly. "Can you keep the cover going?"

She nodded and headed for one of the tables. As she shrugged into her coat, I caught up with her.

"You got everything? Let's get while we can."

As we left, several of our fellow interns called out. Tibby waved at them but neither of us stopped to chat. I could tell that there would be lots of gossip about us tomorrow, but I didn't mind. There were worse things people could say about me.

We didn't speak until we were safely in my car.

"You. Idiot." I turned to her. "Do you realize how close you came to losing everything? That old bitch would have wiped the floor with you!"

"I am an idiot," she admitted. "Thank you so much for saving me from myself and my own stupidity."

"You're welcome. What in the hell were you thinking?"

"I wasn't. Well, I was, but not with my head."

"I swear to hell, you're worse than any guy I know."

"Not really. Just a moment of stupid weakness. Which you, being the amazing friend you are, rescued me from."

"Please try to keep your weakness to yourself. I don't want to have to keep rescuing you from cheesy old guys and their harpy wives."

Tibby shuddered. "She was really awful, wasn't she? I don't know why I didn't realize how awful she was. Not that I have much excuse, but damn."

"Well I'm sure you and Ger didn't chat about the little woman at home."

Tibby rolled my eyes. "We didn't really chat about anything at all."

"Of course you didn't. He's a total tool."

"Thank you, Bryant."

I made a face at her.

"No, seriously," Tibby continued, sounding a lot more together than I thought she was. "Thank you. I think you more than just save me from a tool. I think that old bag would have ruined me."

"I don't know about that. She's got to be used to Gerry screwing around." Although I'd seen her go at secretaries a few times, interns were a little higher up on the ladder at the office. Not much, but even a little bit went a long way.

"No, I think she would have gone for blood with me."

"I don't know for sure, but let's say I do so you stop fucking around with married jackasses."

"Deal. You know the gossip is just rolling through the party right now. You're going to have to pretend to have a mad passion for me for a little while." She grinned to show me that she didn't expect it to be real.

"I can't tell everyone what a crap drunk you are and just be your friend?"

"Well, sure, but you have to wait a couple of weeks to do it. That way, neither of us get any further beady eye from the dragon lady."

"It'll be tough. I'll do it, but you're gonna owe me." I laughed at the idea that we both thought of Mrs. Goodman as a dragon lady.

"What do I owe you?" Now she sounded wary.

"You have to take your bar exam with me and then open our own firm together," I said quickly. Please, please, please don't say no! In spite of all the challenges I'd seen from her this semester, she was still the person I felt would be fantastic. Which made no sense, because working with people who drank too much, or indulged in anything too much never worked out. But Tibby had been my first choice for some time, and nothing had changed that gut feeling.

Not that I'd told anyone about it.

"You're serious?" She asked.

"Absolutely. I'm focused on international, and you are looking at admiralty. We could form a great practice together. All we need to do is get a couple of really solid clients, and we're in."

"So, what was that kiss back there? We've never been like that." She changed the subject.

That was weird. She wanted to talk about my charade when I was asking her to go into business? "It was to throw off the gorgon. No time for her man if you were busy with your own. Plus, you're one of my best friends." I surprised myself by saying that. Until that moment, I hadn't thought of her that way, even though I'd known her since I'd begun law school." I can't let you fuck yourself over," I added.

"That's all it is, though? Nothing more than that?" She didn't sound like she had an opinion one way or the other. This was more careful than I was used to seeing from Tib.

"Do you want it to be more?" I couldn't keep my surprise to myself.

"No, I don't think so. It just took me off guard, and I wanted to make sure that we were clear and there would be no asshurtery or sore feelings tomorrow."

"None at all. I would have made a move before now if there were." Oh, thank holy God and all the saints above. I was so relieved that she didn't expect more from me.

"Well, I didn't think so, but I was so surprised, I had to ask."

I laughed. "Tib, you're great, and good looking, and fun, but you're not my type."

"What the hell does that mean?" This sounded more like the Tibby I was used to.

"It means you have good taste in friends such as myself, but you pick shitty men to date. You also have the complication of being a girl," I added. I didn't look at her.

Her mouth opened, then closed, then opened again. "Wait, are you officially coming out?"

"You don't sound shocked at all," I said dryly.

*T*hat had been it. That had solidified the friendship that was, until that point, only a school-based friendship. She'd gone with me to see Grand-dad, and we'd convinced him to back us, and help us get started opening a new practice.

I always felt that Tibby, in combination with the idea that my dad would be furious I didn't follow him, Casey, and Matt into trial law, was what sold my Granddad, but I never once regretted having Tibby with me.

And then with all the things she'd told me before she and Seth got together—a djinn, and different lives, and all sorts of way-out-there stuff. I almost didn't know whether to believe her, but Seth backed her up.

They couldn't both be on drugs.

I wasn't entirely sure, though, because it sounded too crazy. Until Xavier told me about his brush with the djinn. After he and Olivia got engaged, he, Seth, and I had gone out, and he'd told me that he had met the dude, too. And that he pissed him off, and the djinn took away his memory of the meeting. It was funny—Seth and Tibby were extremely grateful to Dhameer, the djinn in question. Olivia, who was now Xavier's wife, was grateful as well. Only Xavier had some leftover resentment. It made me laugh. That was so Xavier. I could see why the djinn had gotten pissed and left Xavier to his own devices.

Prior to Graham walking out of my life, I'd been happy that Tibby and Xavier were able to find their forever happy. I'd even been smug that I'd found it for myself and didn't wish to see Dhameer. But now—I wondered this djinn had chosen my two best friends and not me. Or, more specifically, with my life in tatters, why hadn't Dhameer the djinn shown up to help me out?

In some ways, they had a lot fewer challenges than I

did. I couldn't even be honest about how I wanted to live my life. I'd lost the love of my life to that lack of honesty. And I had obviously been premature in my smugness.

But in other ways, Tib and X had a truckload of challenge that I would never understand. So maybe they needed the help of a djinn.

I thought about what they'd told me about their wishes. If I could have a wish, it would be for my family to accept me. All of me, just as I was. With Graham, married and building a life together.

I tried to see my brothers being cool with it. They'd been borderline about the fact that I was different most of my life. They were always joking with me about one thing or another, but that kind of joking that left a mark.

My dad? He still held a grudge that I didn't go into the same field of practice. More specifically, his practice. My mom would probably be okay and spend a lot of time soothing the hurt feelings of my male relatives.

Like they were children, or something. I rolled my eyes at the thought.

Granddad was the only one who I thought suspected but didn't care.

"Hello? Earth to Bry?" Tibby was waving a hand in my direction.

"Sorry, I got sidetracked." Her words dragged me from the past and my own sad musings.

"I can see that," she said, her tone dry. "What is it, Bryant? You're like a little kid who has hidden a toad somewhere on your person, and you're not supposed to have it. Additionally, you're dying to spring the thing on people. Until you do, though, you can't sit still. It's fidget, fidget, fidget with you."

I grinned. Although my toad wasn't a surprise, and it wasn't something I was excited about. I had the sinking feeling that the only way I'd get out of this, and get the toad out of my pocket, was to be honest, and in that, Tib was right. I couldn't sit still, thinking about it. I hated it when she was right. Tibby was spot on in her analysis. Not that I'd admit it.

Ever.

"I don't know. My two best friends are leaving me to go somewhere I can't," I said, not wanting to try to make something up. With Tib, I could be honest about where I was. Just because this wasn't *totally* honest…

Tibby's face fell. "I'm not leaving you. Neither is X."

I shrugged. "But there are two more people. And I don't mind!" I held up my hands. "It's just hard to be the fifth in all that."

Tibby looked hard at me. "Are you wallowing?"

It was great to have a friend who I could speak short-hand with. Even if I was skirting the real deal.

"Kinda. You know, the gay best friend thing." I needed to tell her about Graham. I couldn't get the words out.

"Your mom wants grandkids again? Doesn't she get enough with Casey's two monsters?"

Her comment shifted things in an unexpected direction. She'd met my nephew and niece. They were pretty wild. Casey and Melissa, his wife, thought they were 'cute'.

Everyone else tended to tie things down around the kids.

"Apparently, there are never enough. Matt and Pricilla are expecting, too."

"You just got a nine-month reprieve, guy."

"Yeah, but you know I'm never bringing some nice girl home to Mom."

It was Tibby's turn to laugh. "I hate that your mom had the wrong idea about us for so long. I mean, I hate that she was disappointed. I like her even if she's a little old-fashioned."

"She was rooting for you," I grinned at her. "My dad told me to get an ironclad prenup."

Her mouth fell open. "Are you shitting me? The nerve of him!"

"Well, he was worried you'd take me to the cleaners."

"He's not wrong," Tibby smirked.

"Whatever," I drawled, waving a hand at her. "You've never seen the day."

"Who is the partner who does the negotiating?" Her eyebrows went sky high.

"Who goes to court and doesn't piss off judges?" I raised one of mine at her.

"Shut up," she said after a moment, and we both laughed.

"Okay, seriously," she continued. "You have to tell them at some point. You're almost thirty. The granny clock is going to be ticking even more loudly when that switch is flipped, and you're going to find that nothing will be a good answer other than the truth."

"Since work is obviously not going to get done, sure, let's talk about my personal life."

"That's why best friends work together," Tibby said with a hint of smugness in her tone. "We look like we're working. Besides, there's nothing do or die on our to-do lists."

"So you say."

"Hey, unless a tanker runs into something it shouldn't, I'd say we're okay for the next twenty-four hours," Tibby said. "Let's get back to this whole coming out thing. It's not like all your friends don't know. And I really don't know how your family didn't clue in when you three were at a club that catered to the gay community," she finished.

I shrugged. "They chalked it up to us drinking too much and generally blamed X."

"Yeah, I can see where that would be a natural assumption for him."

"And you're right. They are pretty preoccupied with the grandkids." I laced my fingers together. "I don't even want to hear it," I looked out the window, "But I am having a shit day."

"Why?"

"Graham and I…" I stopped, looking at the wall behind her head, steadying myself. "We had a fight."

"About what?"

I shrugged. I wasn't ready to tell her. I felt so small, ashamed. That he would leave me; that he would accept and then reject a proposal in the space of ten minutes. I hadn't proposed to anyone else, and didn't have a lot of experience in this department, but I didn't think this was normal.

Something was very off. I didn't want to think that it was me. But what else could it be? Why couldn't I just say it?

Tibby looked at me intently, hands on her hips. Then she left the room. But in a few moments, she returned carrying two glasses and a bottle. She shut the door behind her, and then set the bottle and glasses down on my desk, and poured us both a shot of her private whiskey stash.

She handed a glass to me. "Drink."

I took it and threw the entire thing back. The whiskey burned my throat, and I could feel it go down into my stomach. It was way too early for this, but I was so glad she'd done it.

"I'm tired, Tib."

"Of what?" She had her arms crossed, the whiskey glass in one hand, and she perched on my desk.

"Of… I don't know. Not feeling as though I can talk to anyone," I finished lamely. "You're the only person who knows the real me."

One eyebrow went upward. "There's a reason for that."

"Oh, come on. No one else has ever taken the time to know me. No one has bothered."

"Have you let them in?"

I hated when she got all work-like on me.

"Did you know that my brothers each dated the entire varsity cheerleading squad in high school?"

"So?"

I could tell that she didn't get the connection. "So I was expected to do the same. They had no idea. And while it's not high school anymore, I'm still expected to be trying to date the cheerleading squad."

"Who wants to date cheerleaders, anyway?" Her nose wrinkled. "Can I do anything to help you in this? Have you talked to him today? Should we invite him out to dinner?"

For a moment I stared at her. Invite who out to dinner?

Then it hit me. She was talking about Graham. She didn't know that he'd left. That it was over. Because I couldn't be honest.

"No, although I wish I could dump this on you. But I have to handle it myself. How in the hell that's going to happen is still a mystery. Enough of my whining. Let's get through this and go meet Seth for dinner."

"Gee, thanks for the invite," Tibby said.

"You're welcome. Quit slacking and get back to work!"

"You just don't want to talk about your current romantic quagmire."

"You can't leave it alone, can you? There's nothing to talk about," I said.

She flipped me the bird as she left. I threw a pencil as she rounded the door.

"Lame," I heard her sing as she went into her own office.

It felt good to get this off my chest, but it did nothing to advance my problems.

Maybe it was time to ask Granddad out for dinner as well.

3

I sat with my grandfather, waiting on Tibby and Seth. I knew they wouldn't mind me inviting him—we all enjoyed being together. Tibby told me Granddad felt like he was hers, too.

"So how's business?" Granddad asked.

"It's good," I said, taking my mind off my personal shit. "We're going to have to hire another paralegal."

"You know, I wasn't sure this was a good choice, when you two came to me," He leaned back in his chair, looking across the restaurant. "But somehow, you have made this a big success. And it's been a good return on my investment!" He winked. "That Tibby, she's a terror. Met one of my friends from another firm that dealt with her recently. Said she nearly made the associate they sent in piss himself."

We both laughed.

"Yeah, she's good at the intimidation side of things."

"You're no slacker yourself. I've seen you in court."

"You have?" I was surprised. "I've never seen you there."

Granddad cut his eyes at me. "Seen all my grandsons. What kind of grandfather do you think I am?" He rolled his eyes, then continued. "I know your dad was disappointed—"

He ignored my snort. 'Disappointed' was putting it mildly. I was supposed to be the last part of his legacy, and part of the triumvirate that would take over his empire. My brothers had already obliged with his ideas for their careers, and he didn't see why I thought I was better than that.

"But you are good at what you do. Calm, quiet, and no one can outdo you in the facts. I've seen them try."

I smiled, trying not to look smug. "I've never lost when we've had to go to court."

"I know. So far, you're the only Higgs who can say that."

"It's good to see that someone else besides me knows that, Granddad."

Something in my tone must have alerted him. He looked over, and his expression was serious. "I know your dad doesn't understand a lot of why you do what you do. But he loves you. He just…"

I sighed. "He's just who he is. Yeah, I know, Granddad. I'm a little tired of having to always make allowances for it. I'd like to be who I am and not have to—"

The beginning of what could have been a tirade, or the complete truth, was cut off by the appearance of Tibby and Seth.

Which was probably a good thing. When it came right down to it did I really want to get into it, even with Granddad? My completely honest self said no, I was afraid to tell even him. What if he rejected me?

A part of me was tired, really tired, of being afraid all

the time. But if I wanted things to be different, I'd have to fix them.

It didn't feel like I had the bandwidth for that at the moment.

After dinner, I headed home. The townhouse was dark, and it felt cold, even though it wasn't.

I knew why it felt that way. It was because Graham was gone.

It had been four years since he'd come into my life, and without warning, with no transition—he was gone.

He wasn't coming back. My mind went back to last night. When the door had closed behind him as he left our home—I'd closed a door on everything that had happened. But for whatever reason, tonight the door was kicked open, and I couldn't close it again.

I'd have to go through it. I'd hoped to avoid this for a few more days, but no such luck. I closed my eyes, and bracing for the pain I'd avoided last night, thought through all that happened.

Not only was it my birthday, but I'd asked him to marry me. All day, I'd thought about how I was going to do it, and how excited I was to hear him say yes. He accepted, and for ten minutes, I'd been happier than I'd ever been in my life.

Then Graham asked about what time we were leaving for my family birthday dinner.

"Well, I don't think you should come, Graham." I felt uneasy about saying this, but he knew how they were. There was no way I could tell them about us like this. They had to be prepared. I needed to give them time. I needed to give me time.

I was so busy working out how I needed to make all of this happen I missed the one-hundred-eighty-degree change in Graham.

"What do you mean, I can't come?" His blond hair was messy, and his eyes, normally calm, were glittering with anger.

"You know how they are—" I began.

"No, I don't! I don't give a rat's ass how they are. That won't work anymore, Bryant. This is on you. I know how you are! I don't really know your family. As far as they know, I'm your friend, just your roommate! Did you know your mom said it was nice you were able to find someone to split expenses once Tibby finally moved out? What the hell? I'm your boyfriend! We're together! Except when you're with your family, which is often, since they, you know, live in the same city! Then it's, Sorry Graham, you understand Graham," he mimicked me. "That's not good enough anymore, Bry!" He glared, crossing his arms.

"I don't know what you want me to say," I began.

"I want you to be yourself and be honest with the people in your life about who you are. That means telling them about me. Especially now. Am I supposed to pretend that we still are just roommates that we aren't engaged? You're seriously telling me I'm supposed to pretend all this—" he gestured to indicate my proposal, "Didn't happen?"

If there was one thing I hated, it was an ultimatum. While Graham didn't say it explicitly, this felt like one.

I didn't respond right away, and he said, "I won't live like this anymore. I've given you so many chances, and I understand why you don't feel you're ready. But I can't live this way. So since you can't change, I'm going to have to."

"What do you mean?" I could feel the fear slithering around in my stomach. I was pretty sure I knew what this meant, but I had to hear it.

"I'm done, Bry. I love you, but I love myself, and I hate myself for where I've allowed you to put me. I wish it wasn't like this, but I can't live with myself anymore. Which means I can't live with you."

He looked at me expectantly, and when I didn't move, didn't say anything, he turned without a word.

"I am not going to marry you when you don't even tell your mom that I'm more to you than your roommate, Bryant. Even now, when you've just proposed, there's no truth in it." He walked out of our room with a suitcase in his hand. "I can't and won't be part of that.

I love you, but I can't live a lie for you any longer, no matter how much I love you."

"Did you already have that packed?" I pointed at the suitcase. I'd asked him to marry me and he had a damn suitcase packed?

"I knew we'd be talking about your birthday tonight, and I decided I wasn't going to be kept in the closet with you again. I don't mean to be an asshole, but I can't live like this. I do love you, and I've always wanted to marry you."

"Wait a second. You said yes. But now you're saying no?" I couldn't wrap my head around this. Whatever was happening was happening too fast.

"I thought you proposing meant that you were going to tell your family. That we'd make the announcement tonight. It's not like they don't know who I am." He glared.

"I need to tell them about me, and then I can tell them about us," I said.

Graham looked at me, and I couldn't tell what he was thinking. I could barely tell what I was thinking.

Then he turned, and walked toward the front door, opening it. He looked over his shoulder at me, and then inhaled deeply, and walked out.

He didn't slam the door of the front room behind him. He just left.

I listened, waiting to hear his tread on the stairs, to know that he was headed up to the loft, to have some time alone.

Instead, I heard bumping around out in the hall, in the foyer.

Then the slam of the front door.

He'd left?

Mobilized, I ran for the other room to look out the window. Graham and someone whose face I couldn't see were loading suitcases into the trunk of the car. The other man slammed the lid. Then they both got into the car.

Graham never looked back.

Happy birthday to me, right?

I hadn't seen him since. I didn't call because what could I say? I knew why he was upset, and I understood it. But I wasn't ready? Able? To do anything on my part.

Not to mention, I had a sneaking suspicion that I was going to have to own some serious fuck-ups. Because Graham was right. I'd asked him to marry me, and told him to stay home, stay hidden.

Shame washed over me. What the fuck was wrong with me? No wonder I didn't want to think about this. I knew there was more. But I could only take it a little at a time.

Which should tell me something. This was my fault.

"What the hell?" I asked the empty room as I went to the fridge and got out a beer. I knew that I was in the wrong here, but then why did he say yes and then no? That fact was the one that was going to make me crazy.

"What the hell indeed?" A deep voice asked.

I whirled around. A man—a painted man—hovered in the shadows.

I knew who it was. At least, I was pretty sure I knew. I'd heard of him. But seeing him… it was more than I'd expected. I realized in that instant that in spite of all that Tibby and Xavier told me, part of me didn't believe.

Kind of hard to dispute them now.

"What are you doing here?" I finally managed.

He moved forward, and he was, in fact, hovering. He didn't seem to have any legs. His arms were crossed, and I could see that he was appraising me as much as I was him.

He was hot. Something no one had bothered to mention, but I guess that wasn't on their radar. He reminded me of a deadly blade. Beautiful to look at but would kill you as easily as he would look at you.

"You don't seem surprised to see me. I presume your friends have mentioned me," he said, the barest hint of a smile on his lips.

"Well, I was wondering if I would. Since you're moving down the line of people Tibby knows."

He held up a finger. "No. Of the people Tabitha loves. There's a difference."

I sat down on my sofa, taking a drink of my beer. "Yes, there is." She didn't love many people.

"And I heard your thoughts, full of sadness and woe at what you see as your…" he paused, considering his words. "Plight."

"You don't see it as such?"

He had such a formal way of speaking that I found myself slipping into it. Kind of like being in court and putting on your legal vocabulary.

"I think, like your friends, what you see as suffering has been brought about via your own actions. And while you are in pain now, you are not as poorly as you could be."

"Such as?" Floating hot djinn he might be, but he didn't know me.

"I know you better than you think," Dhameer said.

Because this couldn't be anyone other than Dhameer.

"Really?"

"Yes. You are alone now because your last partner moved out. He left because you are not honest, Bryant Higgs. You are not honest with yourself, or your family— you hide who you are. And it keeps you from getting the things you want."

"I pretty much have everything I want," I said, before I could help myself.

"Oh? That's why you're looking around your home sadly? Lost in memories?" He laughed. "Please, tell me more of this. Feel free to throw in the commentary as to how happy you are."

"Did you come here just to mess with me?" I wanted to be surly, but it all seemed to take too much effort.

"Why do you all ask that? No, I am here to offer you a gift, to help you. I like you, based on what I have seen in how you interact with both Tabitha and Xavier. I like you enough to offer you a wish. The thing you really wish for, what you want in your secret heart, where no one else sees."

"What do I want?" I asked, curious to see what he'd say.

"Love. Acceptance. Freedom. All three of these things are lacking in your life. As I said before, that's due in great part to your actions, but that doesn't change the fact they are not here. Or that you want them."

I took another drink. He was right. Not that I wanted to hear it.

"I can't," I said, and I wasn't sure which part of his statement I was addressing.

Dhameer looked sad, but his words didn't falter. "I can offer you all of those things, and the ability to be with the one person you're supposed to be with, but in order to have that, and him, you need to be open and welcoming. You're neither at the moment."

"How am I supposed to do that? Is that the catch?"

He smiled. "There is always a catch, isn't there? I almost didn't come to visit you. What you want—it's not overly difficult. I don't need to reorder time, or make all manner of crazy things happen so that you can attain the things you want, the life you desire. You have the ability."

"So why are you here?"

"Because I hate to see people suffer who could solve their own problems. Sometimes it takes hearing it from someone not involved."

"I don't get a wish, then?"

"You will get your wish, provided you put in the effort for it to happen. I'm not going to grant a wish so that you can end up here alone, drinking." He rolled his eyes. "I have a tad more pride in my work than that, Bryant."

If I didn't know better, I'd say I'd had too much to drink at dinner. But I hadn't. This was surreal.

"So what do I have to do?"

Now Dhameer rolled his eyes. "Did you not speak with Tabitha and Xavier? There is nothing that is completely free. With djinn this is especially true. You can have your wish—if you do the things that will allow for your wish to happen."

"Okay, so what do I have to do?" Tibby had said he was really clever. I didn't see it.

"That is for you to figure out," Dhameer smiled in a way that suggested more satisfaction than was necessary.

I thought about it. "What—wait! I have to fix things, and not only that, I need to figure out what's wrong so that I can fix them—and only then, will my wish come true?"

"No, only then will you have the chance to attain your wish. As with your friends, your actions will direct this. Humans, I have found, do not value that which they do not work for." He looked over my head, and I could see a flash of sadness cross his face. It was the most emotion I'd seen from him since he popped up in my house.

"Is that even a wish?"

Dhameer threw up his hands. "You are offered a chance. That's more than most ever get—an assured chance—"

I held up my own hand. "Yeah, if and only I meet some standards, some expectations—"

"Then I withdraw my offer," Dhameer said. His face was expressionless, closed.

I felt my stomach curl in fear. "No, wait!" Tibby would kill me. So would Xavier. I didn't want to tell them I'd finally seen the guy and tossed the offer in his face. Particularly as I was bitching to myself about not getting a wish earlier. They thought the world of Dhameer, and he'd put them both through the ringer.

Dhameer was already drifting away. Would he go through the wall, like a ghost? I wondered.

"Yes?" He looked over his shoulder, dismissive and aloof.

"I'm sorry."

The only movement from him was the raising of a brow that indicated extreme disbelief.

As an attorney, you looked for these small movements, these little bits of physical language that told you the real truth, the real what of what was going on.

I understood silent communication well.

"I really am sorry. I'm not in the best place, and I'm kind of being an asshole to everyone around me."

Dhameer turned around and faced me. "Indeed. Then you are telling me you will accept my offer?"

I nodded. "Figure out what I need to fix, fix it, and then my wish happens."

"You need the time to figure out what you truly wish for, Bryant."

I dismissed that. "I know what that is. That's the easiest part of this whole thing."

The brow went to his forehead.

"I know what I want," I said firmly. I wanted Graham back. I would shout about us from the rooftops if I needed to. He'd been gone less than a day and I could feel the difference in the place.

"Very well. Do we have an agreement?"

"We do."

Dhameer nodded, and then said, "Good luck, Bryant. You do not have an easy path before you, but if all goes well, then you will end up as happy as the friends you cherish."

I opened my mouth, then closed it. I wanted that. Before Graham walked out, I thought I had it, and felt lucky I hadn't needed the help from a djinn, or genie, or whatever he was. Now, when I saw either of my best friends with their spouses, my heart ached. I wanted what they had, and if I had to work to get it back, then that's what I would do.

"Thank you," I said.

Another nod, and Dhameer vanished.

Leaving the glitter that was apparently his trademark.

I sat back down, reaching for my beer, taking a long drink.

Holy shit, did I have a long list of things to do. I didn't even know where to begin it.

I finished my beer, getting up to toss the bottle. Better to go to bed. Plenty of time to focus on this with a fresh head, and emotions that weren't all over the damn place.

4

"Graham, baby?" I reached over, my eyes still closed. Too sleepy to open them.

My hand went out, and I felt the pillow. Where was he?

It was cold, and I couldn't feel a dent in it, or the residual warmth that would be there had he just gotten up.

I ran my hand down his side of the bed. It was cold, too, and the bedclothes still neat. I remembered the last forty-eight hours.

He was gone.

The hot tears fell down my cheek and wet the pillow. I didn't open my eyes. If I did, I would see the empty space, and that would make it real.

I woke before my alarm went off. Was last night real? Had I really seen Dhameer, or was he merely a hallucination?

I knew that Graham was gone. My eyes had the gritty

feel that comes from tears, and now, in the dawning light, I could see the neat side of the bed.

He was still gone.

The bed nearly undid me with each glance. So I got up and headed for a hot shower. I thought better in the shower, anyway.

There was no time to waste. I needed to fix the things that weren't right, and then he and I would be together again. This would be a shitty chapter in our history.

However, that didn't stop a few more tears in the shower. Along with the voice that sounded a lot like my dad's, telling me that men didn't cry.

I really wanted to tell him he was wrong.

Damn it.

*W*hen I got to work, Tibby was already there. I stuck my head in her office.

"Hey, you make coffee?"

Because dear lord did I need it today.

"Yeah, and I even brought in the creamer you like. I figured you'd need plenty of coffee after the family celebrations last night—holy shit, Bry, what is going on?"

Tibby looked up at me.

I opened my mouth, but I didn't know what to say. How to make this *not* a big deal?

She was up and to me before I could figure out what I wanted to share. "What did they do now?"

She knew my family well. She also knew I'd been dreading dinner with them.

"It wasn't them," I said quietly.

"What, then?" Her tone sounded fierce.

Tibby always told me that I'd rescued her from a world

of shit—now that I knew about her wishes, I understood, sort of, what she meant. It was hard to follow all that had happened. I couldn't keep track of where she'd been, or how she'd lived multiple lives. She said she did, and I left it at that. The truth was, while I'd rescued her from Gerry the jerk, she'd rescued me as well. Other than Graham, there was no one who loved me like Tibby. Unapologetically, completely, and fiercely.

Well, now there was only Tibby.

"Graham left," I began.

"Why now?"

Her question startled me. "What do you mean?"

Tibby pursed her lips. "He's been unhappy for a while, but he loves you, so…" she held up her hands helplessly. "He wanted you to work things out for the two of you without nagging."

"He talked to you about this?"

Tibby frowned. "Well, yeah. We're friends, Bry. I mean, I'm not as close to him as I am to you—that would never happen. But he and I were friends. You guys have been together for a long time."

"Not anymore, I think," I said.

"Why?"

"Because he wanted to come with me last night."

"Oh." Her tone said it all.

Tibby, like Graham, felt I should be honest with my family. However, Tibby also understood why I wasn't. She had her own crappy family, and I think she won in the crappy family department between the two of us.

The difference was, she was honest with her family. Her parents' drinking had quietly but definitively torn her family apart. Because of that, she kept her distance, and she wasn't shy about telling them so. They didn't care for it at all.

"Because it will force them to look at their own shit," Tibby always said.

Her sigh brought me back to the here and now.

"What did you tell him?"

"I told him no, of course," I said. I held up a hand to stop the lecture. "I know, I know! I was an ass, and I need to fix it."

"Fix what? Which part? How?"

"Enough with the questions, woman! Have you no decency? It's not even 8:30 in the morning, and I am as yet un-coffeed."

"Fine, you big chicken. Go get your coffee and hide out until I'm taking a break and come looking for you."

As with Dhameer last night, I knew when to not look a gift horse in the mouth. I smiled and practically ran from the room.

Once I collected the much-discussed coffee with my favorite creamer, I hid in my office.

With the door closed.

---

*T*hankfully, Tibby didn't come and find me until nearly the end of the day. We both had a lot of work. Seth's grandfather was getting ready to retire, and he was transferring the entire business to Seth. He was an only child, so there was no one who could protest. I think there were some cousins, but none of them were interested in the old man's business except Seth.

So while there were no personal complications—I envied him with the burning of a thousand suns on that aspect—there was a ton of work to do. Seth's grandfather had been around for years. His business was complex and tangled.

There was also the complication that he had his own attorney, an old boyfriend of Tibby's. Which meant that Seth was in our office more than we were used to seeing him, even given that he and Tib were married.

"He was my first love," Tibby said after the first time Seth had shown up. "Rick, I mean. Not Seth. Seth knows that. He also knows that Rick is happily married and has no interest in me other than an old friend. But that doesn't stop Seth from being all caveman-like," she rolled her eyes, although I could tell that it really didn't bother her one bit.

"You avoided me at lunch, so let's finish this up, and get out of here early so we can go and talk," Tibby stood in front of me with hands on hips.

Shit. "You're not going to take no for an answer, are you?" I asked.

"Nope. It's for your own good," she mimicked my tone of voice. "Remember when you laughed at me for hiding out after we met Seth and Rick? Yeah, well, payback's a bitch, my friend," she grinned.

"You have no pity in you at all, evil woman."

"Not a drop. Finish up. I'm going to save you from yourself."

"What, you're done?" I ignored her saving you comment.

"Totally," Tibby was smug. "I'm always done before you."

I balled up a piece of paper and threw it at her. "Get out of here. I'll come over in a bit. I'm almost done, Miss Smarty Pants."

"Don't sit in here trying to avoid me, either," she said as she left.

I grinned. She had definitely rescued me. It would be for my own good to hang out with her. Not that I'd tell her that today.

Tomorrow, maybe.

---

*W*e ended up going to a bar around the corner from our office. Tibby thankfully waited until we'd sat down and gotten a drink before going into information gathering mode.

"Okay, spill. And don't leave shit out because you know I'll know."

In all honesty, I didn't know where to start. Strangely, I didn't want to tell her about Dhameer. The tasks that he'd given me were lacking in any sort of organization, and they certainly weren't straightforward. From what Tibby had told me, she'd had a pretty clear task. So had Xavier even though he hadn't remembered it. He had to get out of his own way.

Although given who Xavier was that only *sounded* easy. I'd argued with him a few times. 'Stubborn' didn't even begin to cover it. So getting out of his own was a mammoth task. Like me, there were no direct paths, or plans. You had to figure out when you were in your own way.

Maybe each of us had an equally hard task. In my sulking, I didn't want to consider that, but the lawyer in me insisted.

"Well?" Tibby asked with some impatience.

"I'm thinking. There's a lot to unpack," I said, trying to find the right way to tell the story. Without mentioning Dhameer. "So I told Graham the family dinner was last night a couple of weeks ago. He gave me a funny look but didn't say anything. I said something that was probably inane and meaningless, and I forgot about it until earlier this week." I hadn't forgotten, but I'd hoped he had.

And that he would be distracted once I'd proposed.

"What happened?"

"We were talking, and he said he wanted to spend my birthday with me." Everyone who knew me knew that my mom had a rule we spent birthdays together. Tibby had come for a number of years, but she hadn't been around last night.

"I said that I wanted to spend all my birthdays with him, and…" I took a deep breath. "I asked him to marry me."

"What? Wait, stop right there! You proposed to him? And you didn't tell me? What kind of best friend are you? You didn't even tell me you were thinking about it!" Tibby glared.

"I had been thinking about it, but I was nervous and until that day, I hadn't decided whether I would do it." I sighed. "It was all good, at first. He looked at me and he didn't say anything, then he shouted yes and threw his arms around me. So we were laughing and hugging and kissing, and then he asked me about dinner." I sighed. "I told him that I'd see him when I got home. He glared at me, and said he wanted to spend the entire evening with me, not the leftovers."

"Ooh," Tibby said. "That was direct. And harsh."

"Yeah, so I said, well, no, I can't, or something like that, and then he went off."

"What did he say?"

I thought about it. I'd been shocked. Graham was normally so calm about dealing with emotions. But he'd yelled. One of the things he'd said rang with clarity in my head.

"Don't you try to placate me! You're never going to tell your family about me, about us! Do they even know, for real, like, without a doubt, because they've heard it from you, that you're gay? That I am

a lot more than your roommate? The last time your dad came here, he treated me like someone who was lucky that you were letting me live here! Like I was a charity case!"

My dad had been kind of a jerk. Well, a big jerk. I winced. There was no way I'd ever stop feeling bad about that.

"I'm just not—"

"Whatever, Bryant. You're never ready, even though it hurts me, hurts us, and it hurts you. I've been waiting and hoping that you'd finally demand the decency your family should give you. That you'd finally decide it was okay to be honest with yourself about who you are."

I cut him off. "What the hell does that mean? I know who I am! I've always been honest about it! I never lied to you!"

"Yeah, but does your family know?" He grinned at me, and I could see we'd moved way past a normal argument between couples. This was the grin of someone who wanted to draw blood, wanted to win. Who didn't care how much blood was left on the floor.

"That's what I thought. You deliberately keep them in the dark, because it would disrupt your life, this cozy, perfect, well-ordered life of yours. Can't upset the Higgs, can we? Oh no, not that! Well, I'm done with this shit." He took a breath, looking out the window.

"Either you take me with you tonight, and you tell them the truth, or we are done."

"What?" I said. I couldn't believe he'd just laid down an ultimatum.

"You heard me. You've had four years to find some courage. So it's now or never, Bry."

In my nickname, I heard all the love we'd shared, and our history, and the life we'd built. He didn't want this, no more than I did.

"I just need some time, Graham. I'm ready, I think."

His lips tightened, and it was like a wall went up between us. He stared at me for a moment—an eternity—and then said, "Goodbye, Bryant."

"So that was it," I finished, looking at Tibby. "He left.

He was ready. He had suitcases packed, and he went down the stairs and there was someone waiting for him. I asked him to marry me, and after he said yes, he said no and left."

"He called a cab? When?"

I shook my head. "No, it was a friend, or something. I didn't recognize the car."

There it was. The shiver of fear I'd been avoiding since I saw the car that night. That not only had Graham dumped me, but he'd also set things up so he could leave with a clear conscience, and that worse, there was someone else.

That was the real reason I hadn't let Dhameer float out of my living room last night. Because if I could get what I wanted, what I feared couldn't be true.

There couldn't be anyone else if we were meant to be together. Otherwise, what good would it be to promise me that I'd get my wish?

"Wow," Tibby said. "Well, I guess he knew what you'd say, didn't he?"

"You don't just spring that one someone," I objected. "But I can understand why he did it. He was frustrated." Now I was defending Graham?

I didn't want things to work out with us and then there be weirdness between him and my friends. Because my friends were my family.

"Although I don't know why he worries about them so much. You guys are the family I really care about."

"No," Tibby shook her head. "No, we're the family that knows you and loves you, and accepts all the things that make you, you. Your blood family doesn't do any of that, and in spite of you choosing your friends as a family, you still spend a lot of time with your actual family."

"I do not," I said, almost automatically.

"Yes, indeed you do. They are more important than you give them credit for. You have dinner at least once a month, and there are a million birthdays that you go to. I don't know how that's possible, since there are not a million of you, but it is. You're with them a couple of times a month, and you go out with Granddad more than that."

"Do I really see them that much?"

She nodded. "So that's at least two, if not more, things that Graham doesn't get to go to. Let me guess," she rolled her eyes. "He's just the roomie?"

"Yeah," I sighed, feeling deflated. "The last time he was over, my dad was pretty shitty to him."

"I hate to say this, because you know I love you, but I kind of understand why Graham said and did the things he did. Not the whole proposal thing!" She added. "That was shitty. But he mentioned his frustration to me. Not a lot!" She took my hand across the table. "But he was honest enough that I knew what he meant." She let go of me and took a sip of her drink. "Why don't you just tell them?"

"No one gets this! You know them, Tib!"

"I know. They wouldn't kick you out, and if they did, who cares?"

"Because they're my family!"

"I thought your friends were your family that mattered," Tibby said slyly.

"Damn it," I muttered. She'd caught me in my own web.

As annoying as it was, my family was important. And Graham had seen that. I looked up at her, feeling extremely sorry for myself. "He was right to push me, wasn't he?"

She nodded.

"Damn it," I said again.

Well, at least now I had a better idea of what I needed to do. Well, I'd kind of known, but this solidified it.

"I guess I need to see who's up for dinner next weekend," I sighed.

"It'll be better to get it out in the open, once and for all. Who wants to spend their life hiding?" Tibby asked.

Who, indeed?

5

*W*hile I might be king, queen, and entire royal family of avoidance at times, once I'd decided on a path, I didn't hesitate. That got nothing done.

The next day, I called my mom.

"Bryant!" She answered on the second ring and sounded pleased to hear from me. "During the week? What's going on?"

"I wanted to see if everyone was getting together this weekend," I said.

"Darling, I think I can put it together. Do you want to go out?"

"No, I'd like to have everyone over, if that's all right?" I wanted to be home, on my own turf, where I felt safe. I had to restrain from shouting, *Hell no!* to Mom.

"Oh, that would be wonderful! You haven't cooked for us for a while. What can I do to help?"

My mom really was awesome. "Just call and get everyone on board. How about late Saturday afternoon?"

"I think that can happen," Mom said. "Let me make

the calls, and then you can let me know if there is anything else I can do."

Mom loved to entertain, either for herself or others. Hated to cook, which is why she really liked when I did.

"Okay, Mom. I'll let you help me plan the menu. But first, let me know how many people I'll need to plan for."

"All right, darling. Talk to you later." She hung up.

How long had it been since I'd invited my family over? Not for some time. Not after Graham moved in after Tibby officially moved out.

Because it would mean explaining things I didn't want to.

The mere thought of my dad and how he'd behaved made me cringe again.

I picked up the phone and dialed Graham.

"Hey," I said to his voice mail. "I… I don't know what to say. I miss you. I wish you'd come home, but… I guess… I understand why you left. I couldn't see who picked you up. I'd like to talk to you," I hurried to add. "Please. Call me back. Please." I stopped, not wanting to break down. "Please. I love you."

Then I hung up. I had so much I wanted to say to him.

I hoped it wasn't too late to have him listen. But it couldn't be!

Dhameer said I'd get my wish. This was my wish. I just had to fix things, and I'd get my wish.

This had to work.

If this didn't work, I know what I would do. My goal was to get my life back. The end game was to get Graham back. If that meant I had to come out to my family that was what I needed to do.

Sighing again, I got up and went to Tibby's office.

"Hey," I said.

She looked up. "What's up?"

"So I have the process in motion," I said. "Are you and Seth around for dinner this weekend?"

Her eyes widened. "You're really going to do it?"

I nodded. "Yeah, I think I am."

"Where?"

"At my place. I'm cooking."

"You want some help?"

"Oh, God, please!"

Tibby laughed. "I'll be delighted. So will Seth."

"You sure you don't need to check with him?"

"Nope. He'll be as thrilled for you as I am."

"Well, okay, if you're sure. I'll let you know what time."

"Okay," she said. "Anything else?"

"No, I think that's it. As far as life-changing announcements that will be forthcoming."

"Well, good. More than one a week is just more than I can handle."

"Shut up," I said. And I walked back to my office.

At least I knew I would have allies with me. Regardless of what my family might do, Seth and Tibby will be there supporting me.

It was weird. I've been pretty open with my friends, after a period of assessment. When I figured out that they were trustworthy, I'd let them know. It had never been that big of a deal for me. Only with my family Only with my family had the idea of who I wanted to date and spend my life with become like the sword hanging over my head.

In spite of the fact that I had work waiting for me, I spent some time figuring out the menu and the shopping list. I liked to cook. It gave me a sense of control of my environment. Given the purpose of this dinner, me having any sense of control was probably a good thing.

Once I finish my list, I set thoughts of this weekend's

plans. Aside and got back to work. Stewing over it wouldn't make anything better.

$\mathcal{T}$he week went quicker than I thought it would. Before I realized it, it was Friday, and I was heading to the grocery store to do with my shopping. My mother had been so excited that I was cooking, she apparently hounded every member of the family into accepting. So everyone would be there.

I supposed that was good. I'd get it over all at once, and everyone would hear it for me. As I was leaving the grocery store, my phone rang.

It was Graham's ring tone.

"Hello?"

A slight pause, and then Graham spoke. "I got your message," he said.

"I'm glad you called me back."

"What did you want to talk about?"

"Can we meet this weekend? I'd love to talk to you," I said.

I didn't start the car because I felt like I needed to put all of my attention into this phone call. I couldn't even have the distraction of driving.

"I don't know, Bryant," he said.

"I'd love to get together on Sunday. If you have time?"

"Does it have to be Sunday?"

Shit.

Graham hated to be boxed in. I had forgotten about that. It meant that I had to leave dates and planning slightly open-ended when I went and spoke with him. But there was no way that I could talk to him on Saturday morning, or afternoon, and then put together a dinner for my family and tell them I was gay. That just wasn't going to happen.

"Yeah, I have a bunch of things to take care of on Saturday. Work is really crazy right now," I added.

I didn't like lying, but I didn't want to get into this. And honestly, according to him, we were no longer together. So I didn't have to give him my entire agenda. I also didn't really like that I fell into using us being broken up as an excuse when it was convenient for me. That was something I'd have to think about.

Later.

"I think Sunday will work, but my plans aren't quite sent to the weekend. Can I call you Saturday?"

For Graham, that was an olive branch. I would take it.

"Yeah, give me a call. Let me know."

"Okay, I will. Talk to you later," Graham said.

I couldn't quite tell what the tone in his voice was. Hesitance? Reserved? Definitely reserved. I suppose I could understand. He was hurt, and he wasn't going to put himself out there to be hurt again.

Although for me personally, I couldn't understand. I didn't like this game playing, but no one was perfect. However, Graham was perfect for me. And this was going to be part of the way that I brought Graham back into my life. Nothing worth having was easy. If this is what it took, this is what I would do.

I couldn't wait for dinner now. Because once I had dinner, and told my family the truth, then I'd be able to focus on putting Graham and I back together.

*S*aturday arrived, and I got up and started prepping my materials. I spent the night before cleaning, making sure that everything looked spotless. Since Tibby had moved out, my house had gotten cleaner. She was the messier of the two of us. Graham and I were on a similar level with regard to cleanliness.

With Graham being gone, I felt like I'd barely been living. So there wasn't tons to clean, but it made me feel better to do it.

I set the table, taking time with all the flatware, and the glassware, and arranged the flowers that I bought at the grocery store last night. I enjoyed entertaining, and in spite of my feeling that this wasn't going to be comfortable tonight, I still wanted everything to look the way I liked.

The doorbell rang, and then the front door opened. When Tibby had moved out, I told her to keep the key, just in case. While Graham was living with me, she had never used it. But I guess now, she wasn't worried about offending him any longer.

The thought gave me pause. While Tibby had never said anything, I wasn't entirely sure that she was as sad for me as I was about Graham leaving. She'd stayed pretty neutral on her own thoughts on him.

Which was what a good friend did.

"Hey," Seth said. "Here we are, you're willing kitchen workers. What can we do to help?"

"Open the wine and let it breathe," Tibby said. She held out her back towards me, a bag that was obviously full of bottles of wine.

When she had moved in with me, she had no sense of wine, or how to pair with a meal. That was one thing I had done.

"It's good to see you haven't forgotten all the things I've taught you," I said with a smile.

"I can be taught," Tibby said.

Seth laughed. "Sometimes," he said.

"Shut it, you," she said.

Together, the three of us worked, putting the finishing touches on the meal. Actually, I did most of the work, while they both drank wine.

That was fine with me. Just having them with me made a difference. The doorbell rang.

"Showtime," I said. I went to the door, and it was my parents, who had also brought Granddad. His driving was getting more erratic these days.

"Bryant, whatever you're cooking, it smells delicious." My mom kissed my cheek.

My dad shook my hand and smiled. He looked happier than normal, and that cheered me up a bit.

"Good to see you, son. Thanks for having us over," he said.

Dad sounded almost casual. It threw me a little. Maybe he'd always sounded casual, and it was just me? I push those thoughts from my head. I didn't need to distract myself with the what-ifs.

"Come on in, let me get you a drink."

They followed me to the kitchen, and Tibby came over to greet them. She gave all three a hug and a kiss, with a longer one to Granddad. Seth shook hands with both my dad and Granddad and hugged my mom.

"What are you drinking?" I asked.

"Don't you have wine prepared for dinner?" My mother teased.

"Well, of course I do. But I always like to pretend to give you a choice."

"No choice needed for me," Granddad grumbled. "I'll have a scotch and leave you all to the wine."

Everyone laughed. The doorbell rang again, and both of my brothers came in with their families. I was pouring wine, getting drinks, and finishing up the last bit of dinner. When we finally sat down to eat, I looked around me with pleasure. It was nice having them here. Why had I never had this level of comfort with them before?

It was because I had never been honest with them before. At least, not like I was about to be now.

Please let them accept this. Please don't let them be assholes. I hated to think that about my family, but I'd heard of too many people who had finally come out to their families, and been shocked at the level of negativity that resulted.

Conversation sort of came to a lull and I decided that it was now or never. I could feel my stomach drop to my shoes, but I stood up and tapped my knife against my wine glass gently, calling attention to me.

"I'm really glad that everyone is here today," I said, looking around, trying to make eye contact with all of them—except the kids, who were preoccupied with half-throwing food back and forth. Oh, well. The tablecloth would wash, and other than that, they were Casey and Melissa's problem.

"I asked everyone here because I wanted to share with you all, and honestly," I grinned, feigning a courage I didn't entirely feel, "I didn't want to have to keep telling everyone individually."

I saw a couple of weighted glances exchanged, but I pretended I didn't.

"On my birthday, I asked the love of my life to get married, and..."

My mom started to cry, smiling at me.

"He said yes."

*C*omplete. Silence.

   That was what I heard. My mom's mouth fell open, and her tears fell down her cheeks as she looked at me.

I couldn't tell what my dad was thinking.

I hurriedly looked at Tibby and Seth, and they both nodded reassuringly at me.

Matt was the first one to speak. "Looks like you need to pay up, Case," he said, directing his words to my other brother, Casey.

Casey smiled. "You did a good job hiding it, Bry. I was sure you were just trying to stay off the Mom radar." He pulled out his wallet and handed Matt a twenty-dollar bill.

"You made a bet?" I asked.

"Had it for years," Matt shrugged. "I'm your brother. I knew."

"And you didn't?" I asked Casey.

This wasn't quite how I wanted it to go, but no one was calling me Satan's Spawn, so I would take it.

"I wasn't sure, and Matt was so smug, you know how he is. I had to bet against him." Casey laughed.

That made Matt and I laugh, too.

Which brought it into stark relief that no one else was saying anything.

"You're gay?" Mom asked.

"You didn't even suspect?" Matt asked her.

She sighed, thinking about it. "Well, I heard from—it doesn't matter now, but I did hear from someone they thought you might be—" she waved her hands dismissively. "I figured what does anyone know? You're my son. So you're engaged?"

Now it was my turn to sigh. "I think so. He insisted I tell you first because he doesn't want to hide our relationship."

I felt, rather than saw, Tibby's start of surprise. I was kind of making things up on the fly, here. Graham hadn't given me an ultimatum with an opening for us. But I knew that once he heard what had happened, he would be open to moving back in, and planning our lives together.

"Well, good that he knows what he wants," Mom smiled. "Have we met him?"

"Yeah, it's Graham," I said, surprised.

"Oh, well, that's good. I like him, he seems a very nice young man. What sort of wedding are you thinking about, dear?"

I wondered had I done my parents a disservice by assuming the worst. My mom sounded just like she had when my brothers told her they were getting married.

"You're gay? You sure about this?" My dad asked.

Apparently, I'd thought too soon.

"Yeah, been pretty sure for a while now, Dad."

He glared at me. "It's not too late to change your mind."

"Why would I want to? I feel better now than I have in a long time. I'm being honest with you, my family."

My dad crossed his arms, sitting back in his seat. "I could have done without knowing it the rest of my days."

It felt like someone had stabbed me in the chest. I'd read a what felt like a thousand coming out stories online once I'd decided to do this. I was starting to feel obsessive, but one of the things I'd told myself was that my family wouldn't be as bad as some I'd read about.

But there was my dad, sounding like one of the families from the stories I'd read.

He turned and looked down the table to Tibby. "Did you know?"

She gave him a what-the-fuck look. "Of course I knew. I've known since law school." Her tone made it clear what she thought of him.

"Did you know?" Dad turned on Granddad now.

Granddad shrugged, taking a drink of his Scotch. "Thought that might be the case. Don't really care though. I can't see what difference it makes. He's a damn fine kid, and good at his job. What else do you want?" He gave Dad a serious side eye. "But if you're asking if Bryant confided in me, and I've kept it from you, no. He did not, and I have not."

"Gene," my mom began.

"No, Marg, don't hush me now. Why haven't you told us before? Do your clients know?"

Now I was mad. "No, Dad, they don't. But they don't need to. I could be green with four arms, and I'd still do a good job for them," I started.

"Mr. Higgs, I would be careful," Tibby chimed in. "Now you're impugning both of us, and our ethics."

I loved her. She always knew where to go for the best hit.

"Stay out of this, missy," my dad snapped at her.

Melissa, Casey's wife, who had been silent until now, burst out. "I can't believe you all!"

Everyone stopped to look at her.

"You're dithering over what this means to clients? What does this mean to us, to this family? To my children?" Her voice rose.

It felt dangerous to me. But I waited to see where she was going even though I was afraid I knew.

"Bryant, I've always liked you. Even loved you, because you're Casey's brother, and I've always thought you were a good man. But now, to know that you're gay?" Her voice rose again, and this time, I was sure it was dangerous. "I do not want my children around a man of such a dubious moral character." She stood up.

"Melissa, what are you saying?" Casey asked, putting a hand on her arm.

She shook it off, almost violently. "I'm saying that this is wrong, and I cannot support this. I won't have this around my family, or my children."

She turned to the children, who had stopped throwing food and were silently watching the interchange between all the adults. "Kids, come on. It's time to go."

"But Mama, we haven't had dessert yet!" Casey Jr, my nephew, said.

Melissa stepped away from the table, heading towards them and making shoeing motions. "That doesn't matter now. We'll get ice cream when we get home. Come on, let's get our things."

Casey Jr and Hannah got up quietly, both looking at me as they did so. I could see the tears shining in both of their eyes because I'd always had a good relationship with my niece and nephew.

"It's okay, guys go on with your mom," I said. "I love

you guys. Thanks for coming to dinner." I smiled at them, attempting to show a confidence I didn't feel.

Melissa didn't even look at me as she ushered the children from the room. Once they disappeared around the corner, she turned and looked at Casey, not meeting the eyes of anyone else at the table. "Casey, let's go."

He shook his head. "You go on, Melissa. I'll catch a ride home with Matt."

"Casey," she began, her hands on her hips.

"No. You're entitled to your opinion, and I respect it, even if I disagree with it. But I'm entitled to mine, and I'm going to stay here with my family, and work this out. I'll see you at home," he turned away from her and back towards everyone at the table.

I felt like crying. This was going downhill fast.

"Casey Higgs, I will speak with you when you get home." She sounded ominous.

Then she walked away, and I could hear her and the kids rustling around and then the slam of the door.

"Yeah, I guess we'll both be speaking when I get home," Casey said grinning halfheartedly at the rest of us. "I'm sorry, Bry."

"It's all right," I said. Not that it felt all right, but he was right. Melissa was entitled to feel however she wanted to feel.

"It's not all right," my dad said. Unlike his normal mannerisms, he and yell, heated bluster, he just stared at the table. Then he looked up, first at me, and then my mother. "Marjorie, let's go home."

She looked at him. "Now, Gene?"

"Yes, now." He stood up. "Thank you for dinner, Bryant. You did a good job as usual. Could've done without the conversation." He set his napkin on the table and walked out of the room. He didn't look back.

It made me think of Graham walking away from me and not looking back as he walked out of our home and into the street. I felt the tears well up in the back of my eyes, I struggled to keep my composure.

My mother stood and came over and put her arms around me to give me a hug and a kiss. "I love you," she said. "And I'm proud of you for telling us. I know it's not easy, and I know he is…" She sighed. "Well, he's not his best right now. But it will all be fine, Bryant."

I hugged her back. "You sure about that, Mom?"

"Yes, I'm sure. It will just take a little time. Thank you for dinner, sweetheart. I love you." Then she stood up. "I'm sorry to be leaving so soon, but I think it's for the best," Mom smiled a little ruefully, and followed my dad out of the room. Then she stopped and turned back towards the table.

"Dad, are you coming with us?"

Granddad shook his head. "No, ma'am, I am not. I am perfectly content to stay here and have dinner with my grandson. Sorry you're leaving."

"How will you get home?" Mom asked.

Granddad waived his cell phone at her. "I can call an Uber like anyone else," he said.

I could hear a bit of laughter around the table at Granddad's comment.

"All right," Mom said. "Love you all, and I guess we'll see you later." She disappeared around the corner.

"Well," Granddad said. "That kind of put a cramp in your entertaining, Bryant. But I'm not complaining. More for me," and he leaned over and grabbed one of the dishes, spooning more potatoes onto his plate.

Priscilla, Matt's wife, finally spoke for the first time. "Thank you for sharing," she said. "I'm glad you trusted us enough to let us know yourself."

I smiled at her, and conversation moved to less controversial topics.

Finally, I could breathe a sigh of relief. While that had been good, and I didn't even know what to think about Melissa, it had gone better than I expected. I was also glad that no one questioned me further on what was going on with Graham. Those would be questions I wasn't able to answer, and I didn't want to lie any more than I had to. Not that I would have to for much longer.

I couldn't wait to tell Graham all about it tomorrow.

---

*a*fter my family had left, and my brothers had given me longer than normal hugs, Tibby and Seth helped me to clean up.

"That wasn't completely shitty," Seth said, drying wine glasses.

"Yeah, partially shitty is so much better," Tibby said, giving him a look.

"It could have gone worse," I said before she could go off on any sort of defense of me or attack on part of my family. "I've been reading coming out stories—"

Tibby interrupted with a laugh. "Always prepared," she said.

"Always," I agreed. "Anyway, some things I've been reading have been horrible. This wasn't what I hoped for, but it was by no means as bad as I'd worried about."

"Melissa was kind of bitchy," Tibby said. "I thought she was about to brain you with something."

"I didn't expect that," I admitted. "It surprised me."

"I think it surprised Casey, too," Seth said. "I feel bad for him. While she wasn't nice to you, he has to go home to her tonight."

"I've never heard her express any kind of negative views about people who are gay," I said. "I think that was the hardest for Casey. It was unexpected. He was definitely pissed."

Where Matt got mad, and let you know it, Casey was more like me, and he got quiet.

Plotting his revenge, usually.

"You're right," I said to Seth. "That's not going to be a happy home anytime soon."

"I feel sorry for the kids," Tibby said. "They were really sad, and I could tell they couldn't understand why Melissa was so mad."

"Well, Casey will set them straight," I said. At least, I hoped so. I felt a bigger pang than expected at the potential loss of time with them, crazy monsters though they were.

Tibby hung the dishtowel she was using on my drying rack. "It's going to be okay, Bry. I have to ask though. Are you glad you did this?"

I thought about it before I answered.

I felt both crappy and good. Like a weight had been lifted off me even though I had some conflict ahead of me.

"Yeah, I'm glad I did it. Why didn't I do this before?" I asked. Because thinking about today, in spite of the bad, it wasn't as bad as I'd imagined.

Had I really been making mountains out of molehills? Had I really screwed things up with Graham because I couldn't see clearly?

I was going to be pissed if that turned out to be the case. But it wouldn't, I reminded myself. Dhameer told me if I faced the things I was avoiding, and fixed the challenges in my life, I'd get my wish.

"Because fear is a powerful motivator," Seth said. "Thanks for dinner, man. It's always good to hang out. I'm sorry some of your family got all assy, but most of them didn't, so that's the good thing."

I smiled at him. Tibby had chosen a good one. "Yeah, you're right. Better to focus on that."

They both hugged me and left.

Which left me wondering why hadn't I told them about Dhameer yet? Because I didn't want to hear it from them? No advice, or discussion, or anything?

I shook my head. I didn't know and didn't want to think about it. I had enough baggage to deal with at the moment without examining my motives in this aspect.

Besides, I needed to check messages, see if Graham had called me back. I hadn't heard from him before everyone started arriving, and rather than carry my phone around with me and die over not being able to check it every two seconds, I'd left it in my office.

Thankfully for my state of mind, I saw that he'd called and left a message. We were on for tomorrow, and he'd chosen one of our favorite cafes. Good.

I got into bed, tired but partially happy. Sure, this hadn't been perfect, but my family hadn't tossed me out, or threatened to shun me or try to "fix" me. And now, I would get my dearest wish.

Tomorrow was going to be awesome, and this weekend would officially go into my 'best weekend of my life' box.

I was smiling when I turned out my light.

7

I got to Café Cordial early. I ordered a coffee and sat down to wait. I hadn't eaten breakfast, and I might be pushing it with the coffee, because I was nervous.

Which I didn't understand. Dhameer had said I'd get my wish—so what was there to be afraid of? Last night had been where the fear was.

My heart leapt as I saw Graham come in. He looked around, saw me, and oddly, glanced over his shoulder, and then made his way to where I sat.

I got up and hugged him.

"Hey," I said.

"Hey. Let me get a coffee," he said, putting his coat on the chair opposite me. I watched him as he went back to the counter and ordered the complicated coffee that he loved. He was like the stereotype of a coffee shop customer, but he loved coffee. I loved that exacting part of him that had to have things as he liked them.

After some discussion, he moved to the end of the counter to wait. I was impatient for him to join me, but I was glad he was getting what he needed so we could talk without being interrupted.

Finally, an age it seemed—he came back and sat with me.

"So what did you want to talk about?" He asked.

I guess we weren't beating around the bush. Well, I could respect that.

"I had dinner with my family last night," I started.

"You do that a couple of times a month," he interrupted. "So?"

"I invited them over to the house, and after dinner, I told them."

"Told them what?"

He wasn't going to make this easy on me. I deserved it. I shouldn't have asked him to marry me without being willing to tell the world. Because that what marriage was, right?

"The truth. That I am gay, and that I asked you to marry me."

Whatever he'd been expecting, that wasn't it. He opened his mouth and then shook his head. "You actually said that? Told them, I'm gay?"

He looked like he didn't believe me.

I couldn't believe that I'd inspired so little confidence in the man I loved, and I felt like a shit.

"I told them that I'd asked the love of my life to marry me and I was lucky as hell because he'd said yes." I smiled, loving how good it felt to say that.

"And what did they say?"

For the first time since Graham and I had fought, since he'd walked out of our home, I saw him. He was leaning forward, and his interest was evident.

"My mom said, you're gay? And I said, yes, I am."

"What else did she say?"

"That she liked you, and then wanted to know what kind of wedding we wanted," I could feel myself beaming, smiling so big that it felt like the smile would fly off my face.

The furrow between Graham's brows wrinkled. "What else? What did everyone else say?"

"My brothers had a bet! Can you believe it? Matt said he knew, Casey said he wasn't sure but had to bet against Matt on principle. Apparently they had the bet going for years." I felt a wave of love for my brothers. In spite of all my fear, they had acted like brothers should.

"Pricilla, Matt's wife, was totally good with it. But Melissa," I sighed. "You know, Casey's wife?"

Graham nodded.

"Well, she didn't take it well. Said she didn't approve although she didn't say why. Probably a good thing, now that I think about it. Anyway, she took the kids and left. Casey stayed. I haven't heard from him today. Did you know," I interrupted my own train of thought, "my mom said someone said something to her about me being gay, and she said, well, if he is, he'll tell me? Can you believe it?"

"It's not a huge surprise to me. People aren't all mean ogres," he said, echoing an argument we'd had before.

"Well," I reached across the table and took one of his hands. He stiffened, so I didn't grip it tightly. "You were right, and I was wrong."

"What did your dad say?"

I sighed. "He wasn't happy, and he left. He didn't yell, or say anything really horrible, he just left. Mom left with him and even though they brought Granddad with them, he said, I'm staying, I'll Uber home." The memory of my grandfather waving his cell at my mom made me laugh a little.

Graham smiled.

"That sounds like it went okay, then."

I nodded. "It did. It went a lot better than I hoped, even though I really wanted everyone to be happy for me, and celebrate with me. But we don't have to worry about that. Once you move back, we'll start planning for the wedding, and people will either come around or they can stay home!"

Graham eased his hand from mine.

"What?" I asked.

"Well, I don't think I want to move back in," he said slowly.

"What do you mean? What's changed, other than for the better?" I felt my cheeks start to get hot.

"I'm glad you told them. You've needed to do that for a long time. I'm glad that this was the thing that pushed you forward, but…" he stopped, and looked away.

Then he looked at me again. "In the week since I moved out—"

"Yes, what's happened in that whole week? That whole, long week, apparently?" I asked, trying not to be an asshole, because I remembered that when he left, he got into someone's car. Someone who was waiting for him.

After I'd asked him to marry me. And he'd said yes. He hadn't made a call or anything between that time and when he walked out with a suitcase in hand. That meant there was someone who was already planning to be there, waiting for him.

"I've been doing a lot of thinking and talking—"

"I bet," I said, and somehow I kept any bitterness from my tone.

"Listen, I was so excited that you proposed!" Graham knew me well, and must have sensed how I was feeling. "I thought that at last, you had decided to move forward with honesty and openness."

"That's why you had a bag packed, and someone waiting to pick you up," I said, unable to contain myself any longer.

"I had my plans ready because I figured we'd have our normal fight about your avoidance in relation to your family. And had you said that you planned to tell your family the truth when you announced our engagement, I would have told him to go on home. But you didn't. You wanted us to get engaged in secret because of your demons. I couldn't do that. Not to me, and not to you."

I started to speak, then closed my mouth. His last comment made me feel bad.

"I love you, and I am so glad you proposed. But I need to think some more. I need some time," Graham continued.

"What is there to think about?"

He shook his head. "I don't want to get into that right now. You'll have to be okay with knowing that I am not ready to just pick up our lives as though the last week didn't happen."

"So much has changed after only a week? I mean, it has. I finally did what you wanted!" I could feel the heat rising in me again. This was not going how I hoped at all. I felt like I was lost and had no way to get out of wherever it was I'd gotten lost. How had this gone so sideways?

"But that doesn't change how I feel about you, or that I want to marry you," I said. "I even came out when I told my family about our engagement, just as you wanted," I added.

Graham held up a hand. "I think it's better if you don't tell anyone else, and ask your family to keep it private," he said.

"Oh, who's heading back to that closet now?" I asked, and I could hear the nasty tone of my voice.

"No, it's not the closet at all," he shot back, equally angry. "It's the 'I'm not sure where or if this relationship is going anywhere' zone, and frankly, Bryant, I have every right to take as much time as I need. It broke my heart that you asked me to marry you on one hand and asked me to keep it secret on the other!"

We'd both leaned in, our voices lowering to that tone that couples used to fight in public.

Which felt like shit. Just as I felt like shit. Like a tornado, my emotions had whirled from anger to shame. I'd done this to him, I'd made him feel this way.

"You're right," I sat back in my seat. "Take all the time you need."

"I don't like telling you this. I was so nervous, I didn't sleep last night. But I have to be honest with you. This has been one of the hardest weeks of my life, Bry."

Hearing him use my nickname nearly undid me.

"I get it," I mumbled.

He didn't say anything and when I looked up at him, I could see the mixture of emotions playing across his face.

"I have to go," he said abruptly and got up.

"Already?" I asked before I could stop myself.

"Yes. There's nothing else to say that won't end up with us fighting, and I don't want that."

"So what now?" I asked.

He sighed, looking down at his feet. Then he met my eyes. "Let's keep it low key. I need some more time. I need to put my feelings in order, and I think I need to keep working on this on my own. I'll call you later this week, okay?"

"Okay," I said, because what else could I say?

Another moment of silence where I looked away, and

then I heard, "See you, Bryant," and his footsteps walking away.

A week after we'd met in the coffee shop, the week that was even longer than the first week after he'd left, Graham had not called.

a month.

One. Whole. Fucking. Month.

It had been a month since I'd talked to Graham. I'd picked up my phone to call him, probably about, oh, a billion times. Every single time, I put the phone down, even after I'd hit his name in my contacts.

He said he would call me when he was ready.

He hadn't called.

Which meant he wasn't ready.

In between wearing out my phone's screen, I'd been pacing. When a week had gone by, and he hadn't called, I called my mom. I'd been bitching to Tibby every day, but calling my mom made it real. I might have cried a little on that call, but only a little.

I wasn't ready to break down in front of her.

I was also making myself crazy with all the reasons why he hadn't called. I knew it wasn't healthy, but I'd gotten stuck on the idea that the guy who picked him up when he'd moved out had something to do with it, and I took to stalking him on social media. Graham had always been a fan, loving to post things with funny captions and hash tags.

But his social media was a bust. I'd noticed that he'd changed his relationship status to 'It's Complicated' and it pissed me off every time I saw it.

Which was daily. Like I said, I knew it wasn't healthy.

I tossed back the covers and hauled myself out of bed. It was a gorgeous day today, and I was going to make the effort to not be such a grumpy bastard. I knew, even though I didn't want to accept it, that I was going to have to deal with the potential fact that Graham would never call me.

My call to my mom had staved off any questions from the family. Thank God, because I didn't think I could stand questions about wedding planning right now.

Melissa was the only one who was holding her ground of lack of acceptance. No one would tell me what she was saying, which meant it was bad. I'd seen that in clients. People didn't want to tell you the really shitty things other people said.

Casey looked miserable when he mentioned her. She hadn't come to our family dinner after my announcement. I felt bad for him, but I couldn't fix his wife, or how she felt.

My dad was not as abrupt as he'd been, but he was gruff, and I sensed that he hadn't totally accepted it. I let it be. He wasn't being hateful to me, so I took that, and worried about the bigger fish I had to fry.

I decided to walk to the office. When I'd gone to Tibby with plans to open a firm together, we'd initially based it out of here, the townhouse. We had the office on the ground floor level, and we lived above and below it. About three years in, we bought a building four blocks away that we used as our office, and she'd started spending more time on her boat. So I'd been able to claim the ground floor again until Tib moved out of the basement for real.

I loved that it was so close but I hadn't walked in ages. I needed it, needed to get out of the house, and try to start moving in some kind of forward direction again. Even though my heart felt like it was lying around busted into a thousand pieces, and I was too tired and too sad to even start to pick them up.

"Damn you!" I yelled at the ceiling. At Graham. At the unfairness of life. At Dhameer.

Dhameer. I hadn't thought of him much in the last month because moping and online stalking with bouts of obsessing over whether I should be jealous had preoccupied me.

But now that I thought of him... "Dhameer! What the hell? You said if I made changes, I'd get my wish! What the hell? Because I sure as hell don't have it! You lied to me!"

I threw my brush across the room. It felt better to throw something. Maybe I needed to go for a run before I went into the office. Because now, I was seething with anger.

I hated it when people lied to me. I am an adult, and I can handle truth, even if it sucks.

I heard a whoosh, and I turned to find Dhameer floating in the air behind me.

"You are upset?" He asked mildly.

Which pissed me off even more.

"Yes, I'm upset! I did what you said I needed to, and my life is even more in the shitter than it was when you showed up! You said my wish would come true, and I can assure you that it is most definitely not coming true!"

"Why do you say that?"

My outburst didn't seem to bother him.

"Because I'm still alone, Graham hasn't come back, I

haven't even heard from him and my sister-in-law seems to have taken complete opposition to me. I put a rift in my family—"

Dhameer held up his hand. "You did no such thing. What your brother's wife chooses to do is not your fault, or your problem to handle. Besides, how do you know your brother isn't handling things?"

"Because he looks like a man haunted every time I see him!"

Dhameer shrugged. "That is the nature of marriage at times. Partners will disagree, and it takes time to work through them. Do not add that to your list of things you feel you need to manage. Let us return to your claim that I have lied to you. What do you base such a statement on?"

"You told me if I fixed the things that were wrong, I'd get my wish!"

He sighed, shaking his head. "You humans always shift things to best work for what you want to believe. I told you that if you did the work, and made things right in your life for it, you would get your wish of love and happiness."

"Yeah, and none of that has happened."

"Are you not happier with your family?"

"Don't pull that crap with me! Yes, I'm happier with my family. But I want to be happy with Graham!"

"Have you considered that Graham has not contacted you because he is not really what you wish for?"

"What? What the hell are you saying? Of course he is what I wish!" I mimicked his formal way of speaking. "He's the man I want to spend my life with! The man I made changes for!"

Dhameer held up a hand again. "I think I might see your problem, Bryant."

"Oh, you're actually going to tell me something?"

He grinned. "Well, perhaps. I am never not a djinn.

We do not deal in direct answers. Remember, a thing given for free is never appreciated as it should be. That counts for knowledge and advice in addition to everything else. But what I want to say to you is that you made these changes for Graham—what have you done for yourself? What changes have you made to make your life better? What are you doing solely for yourself? You cannot make your life revolve around the actions of others. I'd like to give you a piece of advice, as well."

"You make no sense at all," I stared at him. "But sure, add in some more advice that also makes no sense."

"I think you need to turn inward, instead of looking outward. You are focused on what's around you rather than on what is within you."

"Well isn't that just the end all," I began, but I wasn't able to finish.

He vanished, leaving a cloud of glitter in his wake. Damn him. I remembered that was X's biggest complaint. He suspected that Dhameer showed up, without showing himself, and left glitter to be spiteful.

I hadn't told X I thought he might have deserved it. The thought made me smile.

Almost immediately, the smile dropped from my face. I still hadn't told Tibby about him. She would be angry I'd kept this from her.

I went about my morning routine, thinking over what he'd said, and cursing him when I did speak. But I couldn't stop his words from rolling around in my head. Inward. I had to look inward.

Which meant I was focused on the wrong thing. All this time, and I wasn't on the right track.

That pissed me off all over again, and I indulged in a heated conversation about what I'd say to Dhameer with my bathroom mirror.

However, cursing at him in absentia helped, and when I was ready to go, I set out with a heart a tiny bit lighter, and far more determined.

I would tell Tibby about him today and ask for her advice and help. I would block Graham on my social media accounts, so I would stop myself from looking at him. It would probably nearly kill me for a couple of days, at the very least. But looking at him and trying to decipher all the whys that I had wasn't doing a frigging thing for me.

Feeling better than I had all month, I shut the door, and bounded down the steps.

Thank God it was a gorgeous day. I wouldn't have been able to pull this off if it had been rainy.

When I got to the office, I could see that Tibby was already there. Her lime was in the parking lot—I mean, her car. She had an old Volkswagen Thing that she and her dad had fixed up when she was in high school, and she'd had it painted lime green. Her license plate said 'COCONUT' after the song Put the Lime in the Coconut. Seth called it her flying lime, and I thought it was the best descriptor of her car ever.

While the thought of delving into my emotions didn't thrill me, this was about an inward change. Tibby was the best place to start.

"About time," I heard her say as I came in. We were usually the first ones in, because we liked to get things done before the day officially started, before the rest of the staff showed up.

"Good to see you, too," I said in passing as I headed for our kitchen and the coffee pot.

"Wait! What's this?" She got up and followed me in. "Is this actually Bryant and not the miserable bastard I've been seeing for too long?"

"Shut up," I said. "Yeah, it's me. I think, anyway. What do you have on your schedule this morning?"

"Why?"

"Because I want to close the door and talk to you."

"This sounds serious," she frowned.

I sat down and waited for her to settle.

"Okay, I'm braced. Spill."

"I met Dhameer."

"What?" Tibby nearly knocked over her coffee cup. "When? How?"

"He showed up in my house one day, after Graham left."

"What did he say?" She leaned forward in her eagerness. "You will also need to explain why you didn't tell me at any point during the last month, but that can wait."

"That I could get my dearest wish, but that I'd have to make changes."

She studied me, and then she leaned back. "Is that why you finally told your family?"

"Well, that was Graham's big complaint," I didn't try to hide my bitterness from her. We'd been friends for too long. "Not that it seems to have made much of a difference."

"Are you still looking at him online?"

"You'll be happy to know I blocked him, so that I could stop myself," I said.

"That's good. Online stalking never gets you anywhere."

"You never looked? Not after your three wishes, or whatever? You never looked up Seth?"

She grimaced. "I was afraid to. I didn't want to see that he'd married someone I could pick apart. So I can't really give you grief, because the only reason I didn't look was pure fear."

"I don't know how you did it," I shook my head.

"You don't know how intense things were," she said. "If I'd looked, and saw that intensity transferred to others —at the time, I knew I couldn't handle it. Not the reason why I couldn't handle it, just that I couldn't."

"Well, I'm not seeing anything that gives me any clue as to what the fuck is going on," I said. "So I might as well stop torturing myself."

"Excellent motto. But tell me more about Dhameer."

"He actually showed up again. Recently. I told him he was a liar."

Tibby laughed. "He didn't take that well at all, did he?"

"Actually he was totally calm, which pissed me off even more. He said that maybe Graham wasn't my dearest wish, and that I needed to look more inward for changes, because I'd been focusing on the outward things." I felt myself slump, feeling defeated in having to retell this.

What had all my suffering been for?

"Stop moping. He wants you to learn shit for yourself."

"Shut up. You sound like him. 'Humans don't appreciate what they—'"

"Don't earn," Tibby chorused with me. "Yeah, I've heard that once or twice. But he's right. I would have never found out that Seth was who I was supposed to be with, had I not put in some personal time with me."

"I'm tired of me," I said.

"Well, then, why would Graham want to be with you?"

"I hate you sometimes."

"It's a reasonable question."

"I asked him to marry me."

"He's a good looking guy. No one has to accept a proposal just because someone asks," she rolled her eyes at me. "He's not an asshole, and he was good to you. But," she stopped, tapping her lip.

"What?"

"Maybe Dhameer is right. Maybe Graham isn't your dearest wish. With his hint about looking inward, maybe he wants you to be more honest about what your true wish really is."

"Oh, for God's sake," I threw up my hands. "Now it's time for riddles?"

"That's what djinn do. Nothing is easy, or free with them. You can't ever forget that."

I almost said something snarky, and then I stopped. She was right. I couldn't forget that. Dhameer was a good…. guy, being, but he also was a djinn, and there was always a catch. I could remember Tib telling me that when she told me all about him.

"I have been forgetting that," I admitted.

"So, how do you turn all this inward?"

"I don't know. I've been spending so much time—"

"Being a crazy ex," she said.

"Yeah, okay, maybe. Whatever. Shut up. The point is, I don't even know where to start."

"Well, how about you go out to dinner with your dad? Have you even seen your family since you told them?"

"No."

"There's where you start. I can tell you from experience, when you don't have your family shit sorted, it screws up everything from there."

"Tibby, you don't see your family."

"That's because my parents still drink, and the rest of the family enables it. I'm honest with them, and I write, and even send money at times, because that's what they need, but I don't have to invite their baggage into my life.

They are okay with me, and I'm okay with them. That's what's important, Bry."

Tibby told me that she and I were friends in the other life she'd lived, but that she'd screwed it up. I couldn't remember it—the only Tibby I knew was the one I was friends with now. She'd always been healthy with her family and boundaries. Even if she didn't see them.

"I don't know that I can fix whatever it is with my dad or Melissa," I began.

"Fuck Melissa. She's Casey's problem. Her only obligation is to be polite at family gatherings. If she can't be polite, she can stay home."

"That will go over well."

Tibby shrugged. "Who cares? This isn't her deal, and you don't have to deal with whatever is up her ass. Now your dad, while I feel the same about him, he's worth putting more effort into."

"So I can still be a disappointment?"

"I don't think you were the disappointment you think you were or are," she said immediately.

I started to object, but she kept talking.

"You forget that I have been around your family, to the point where they thought I was your girlfriend. I see things you don't. I think your dad is baffled that you'd put in so much more work to build something from scratch. In his mind, he had things all ready for you to just step right into. And you didn't. I also don't think you suffer by comparison to your brothers the way you think you do."

"Really? How long have you thought this?"

"For a while. But you didn't want to hear it, and it's not my place to give you a wake-up call when you don't want one."

"I don't know whether to say thanks, or what the hell," I said.

"Both are fine. You know I love you more than my car."

"Really?"

"Okay, maybe almost as much as my car. Go call your dad. Have lunch with him and Granddad. Give him a chance."

I sighed. "You're right. Thanks."

"No problem. Don't go anywhere though—what else did Dhameer say? And why didn't you tell me about this?"

I shrugged. "I don't know. I wanted to try to process it myself. Get it together, be successful."

"You have been. Maybe that's part of it. You don't see where the success is."

"This is not what I want," I said.

"Isn't it?"

"Shut up," I got up. "You're not a djinn. So you don't get to be a pain in my ass."

"You don't need to be a djinn for that," she said loudly as I left.

I hated to admit it, but she was right. There was a lot of her being right lately. It was a disturbing trend. I picked up the phone and dialed my dad's office.

Two days later, he and I and Granddad were having lunch in his favorite restaurant, and for once, not talking about anything personal. Given all the time I'd been spending on the personal, it was really nice.

Plus, Dad and Granddad were both really good at what they did, and so it was nice to hear how they were working through some of their concerns. You know, without violating client confidences, of course.

A group of men walked by, and Dad looked up. He smiled at one of the men, who looked to be of the same age as Dad.

"Martin," he said.

"Gene," the other man said. "How are you?" His eyes took in Granddad and I. "Mr. Higgs, Bryant," he added, and the way he said my name got my hackles up.

I glanced at Granddad to see if he'd noticed anything, and he had. His eyes had narrowed.

But we waited.

"So I hear you're going to be a grandfather again," Martin said. "Congratulations. It balances out the… disappointment. A little anyway," his eyes took in me once more.

Are you kidding me? Is he saying what I think he's saying?

Dad heard it too. One of his eyebrows cocked. "Thank you. We're very excited to have another one. As for disappointment? What would that be, Martin? It's been a great year for me, both with the firm, and with my family. I couldn't be more pleased." The eyebrow stayed raised.

Almost like he was daring Martin. The question was, would Martin have the balls? Or the stupids to keep going?

"Well, it's a good thing you will have grandchildren from the older two, at least," Martin sniffed.

Oh, he had the stupids.

"Are you insinuating that my son Bryant, who is sitting here, will not have any children? I'm not sure, so pardon me if I am being a bit obtuse in asking." My dad's voice was icy.

"Well, now, in spite of the fact everything is all legal and nice, it's not like he or…" Martin's mouth pinched up in what looked a lot like distaste, "whoever can have children, now can they?"

My dad stood up, drawing himself into a tower of disapproval. "I believe," he said, and it was loud enough for the entire restaurant to hear, if they wanted to.

Which they did, given the number of people who turned around to look. There were a lot of other attorneys here. I knew a fair number of them. Oh, hell. I avoided the gaze of everyone and focused on my dad.

"You are making a fairly direct slur towards my son," Dad said. "I might be incorrect, but I don't think so. If that is the case, Martin, feel free to consult with any other firm who might be willing to work with you, in spite of your outdated and narrow-minded attitude. Good day," As he sat back down, he deliberately moved his chair, putting his back to Martin.

The other men who were with Martin had been edging away as Martin spoke, digging his hole with my dad. Now they glanced at me, and Granddad, and I could see shame written all over them. They were all younger than Martin, I noted. Whether it was shame at being called out, or shame over Martin's words—I didn't know.

Didn't care either.

Martin swelled up like an angry chicken, but one of the other men with him put a hand on his chest, and another one on his shoulder and steered him away. There wasn't a lot you could say without looking like a bigger ass when someone gave you the direct cut like my dad just did.

The whole dining room seemed to hold its breath, and when Martin and his party disappeared into the foyer, the room exhaled, and exploded into conversation.

I looked at my dad. Granddad was smiling a huge cat-that-ate-the-canary smile.

"Thanks, Dad," I said.

"For what?" He wiped at his mouth carefully with the linen napkin. "Martin? Sometimes you have to stop assholes from giving you too much shit."

He focused on his plate, taking another bite, ignoring me and Granddad.

"I still appreciate it," I said.

"Well, I love you. You're my son, and no stupid jack-off

is going to insult you right in front of me. You're ten times the man he ever will be."

I looked down then. If he said another word, I'd start to cry like a baby. My dad had never said anything like that to me that I could remember. Not ever.

"Well, it's about time you admit it, Gene," Granddad said, clapping him on the back. "Thought you might die before you decided to drop the stubborn ass bit. See, Bryant? You thought this would all go south, but look! You just helped your old man get a step or two closer to a human! You should'a come out years ago!" Granddad laughed at himself.

I couldn't help it. Granddad's pleasure, along with the look on my dad's face as he glared at his father—I started to laugh, too.

Dad glared at us both, and then rolled his eyes, and gave up.

The entire room went quiet again as the three of us laughed so hard we couldn't speak.

It was the best lunch I'd had in years.

I couldn't keep the smile off my face as I drove back to the office. I felt like I could take on the world. I couldn't wait to tell Tibby.

I got back and parked in the lot next to our building. The parking lot alone was one of the reasons we'd bought it. Most places around this part of DC didn't have any parking, other than what you could scavenge on the street.

The cloud of all good things was so strong around me that I didn't even notice when I nearly ran over the guy who had stopped to fix something on his bike.

9

"Hey, guy!" A man's voice shouted. It sounded like he was—oh, shit.

I looked up, taking in for the first time the scene in front of me. A man, a bike over on its side, and the afore-mentioned man looked pissed.

"I am so sorry," I stammered. "I wasn't—"

The man waved his hand dismissively. "Yeah, you weren't paying attention. Same old story. You need to start paying attention, buddy. You do realize we're right out in front of…" he stopped and looked around. "Well, how convenient. A lawyer's office? I could just walk in there and you'd be getting my doctor's bills!" He glared at me, and then, in a movement so small I almost missed it, he looked up at our sign again. "How in the hell did I get all the way over here?"

This was not a good situation, but it was hard not to laugh at this guy threatening me with my own practice. Not to mention his odd question. However, you can't ride two horses with only one ass, as Granddad was fond of reminding me. I decided to concentrate on being threatened with myself.

"This guy? He's a real jerk," I said, keeping my grin low-key.

"Then he would be good at suing the hell out of—shit," he said, dropping his head, hands on his hips. He sighed, then looked up.

"I'm sorry for yelling like a crazy person. You're the second person to crash into me today, and my patience is not what it normally is. I'm also apparently out of sorts and totally lost," he added.

That wasn't what I'd been expecting. Then the man smiled and wow. He was gorgeous. Light brown hair, and tall. Fit, as evidenced by his bike apparel. Slightly tan, which told me he probably biked a lot. A wide smile. The most amazing ice blue eyes I'd ever seen. Wow.

"I'm really sorry. Are you all right? It's fine if you want to talk to a lawyer," I said.

"I'm good. No worries. Just not in the greatest mood."

"Are you sure?" Now I was worried this might be some kind of scam.

"Yeah, like I said, no worries."

"Listen, if anything does come up, here, take my card, and give me a call," I said, fishing a card out of my pocket. If this did go south, I wanted to make sure that I had the ability to say I was trying to do the right thing.

He took my card and looked at it. "Bryant Higgs... attorney?" He looked up, a faint smile at the corner of his lips. "I'm sure I was real intimidating, huh?"

I cleared my throat. "Even more so in front of my office." I gestured at the building. "I'll give you some advice for free. Don't ever admit you're out of sorts to someone who you think you might sue."

He looked at the building, and then the card, and then me, and exploded with laughter. It was infectious, and I found that I couldn't hold in my amusement.

He sobered up after a minute, leaning on his bike. Then he held out a hand. "Declan O'Mara. Good to meet you although I'd have preferred it to be less of a collision."

"Bryant, just like the card says. Seriously, will you let me know that everything's good?" I could hear my dad's voice in my head telling us to be careful because as lawyers, people loved to sue us. Like some sort of cosmic justice or something.

"Yeah, but I don't think it's a big deal. But sure, I'll give you a call."

"Thanks. Sorry I—"

"No problem. I'll check in with you, ease your lawyer brain," he laughed a little as he got back on his bike. With a wave, he cycled off.

I stood, staring. I had to be more careful. I shook my head to clear it and went up the stairs into the office.

"How was lunch?" Tibby asked from her desk.

"Glad you asked. It was a banner meal in the annals of Higgs history," I said, throwing myself in a chair.

"Really?" She pushed her laptop away. "Spill."

I recounted the whole thing, and at the end, I couldn't believe it. There were a couple of tears sliding down her face.

"Are you crying?" I asked.

She snatched a tissue from the box on the edge of her desk. "Yes. Leave me alone. I've never heard your dad go off for you. On you, yes. But in your defense like that? Never. You've never told me about it happening, anyway."

"It was pretty impressive."

"Yeah, so I'm crying." She wiped her eyes again.

"That's so great, Bryant. I'm really pleased for you. Isn't this what you hoped for?"

"I just wanted them to not nag me to death, and to not be assholes about my choices. I never even considered something like this." It still seemed surreal. "I wish you could have seen it, Tib."

"Me, too. I can't be so hard on your dad anymore."

"That's all it took?" I got up.

"That's all? This was pretty big!"

"It was. I'm teasing. Listen, my personal life has intruded for long enough this week. I'm getting as bad as you," I teased her a little more.

"Well, it's your turn," Tibby shrugged, and pulled her laptop close again. "But yes, you should work. I'm bringing home all the bacon these days. And being serious for a minute, we do have court next week."

"So?"

"I might have to go with you."

"Why?"

"Because their lead guy is a complete ass, and I want to see you beat him down. Plus, he's got a temper and it will piss him off to see me there." She smiled.

"Ah, he poked the shark, didn't he?"

"Friggen jerk. He did indeed. You don't have to be polite." She scowled at her screen.

"Oh, good. I'll just take my own personal crap out in court."

"You don't think you can have your shit together by then?"

"Girl, please. You have no stones you can cast in that department." I raised my eyebrow at her. I'd put up with her life getting crazy a couple of times and always in good humor.

Tibby laughed. "You're right, but I'm always going to try."

I rolled my eyes as I left.

She was right. It was a good thing to work with your best friend.

I didn't think about Declan O'Mara until the end of the week when my phone rang. I answered, "Bryant Higgs," without taking my eyes off my paperwork in front of me.

So irritating to still deal with paper when it was much easier to go digital for most of this.

"Bike crasher Declan O'Mara here. Checking in as promised."

Oh, shit. He was calling to tell me that he'd discovered some major injury. The call to my dad was going to suck.

"Hi, Declan. How are you doing?" That was a loaded question.

"I wanted to let you know that I'm great."

"You are?" I asked, breathing a sigh of relief. I hoped I was quiet about it. "That's great," I said, feeling a little foolish. "I'm glad you didn't get hurt because I was lost in space."

"I'm good. But since you're still wallowing in guilt, let me help you deal with that. You can meet me for a beer tonight, and it's all on your tab."

I stilled. Was this a date? It sure as hell sounded like a date. Was he interested? I hadn't gotten that vibe when we bumped into each other, but… it sounded like he was interested now.

It had been a while since I'd been out on a date with someone I didn't know. Graham and I did date nights and

—Graham! I was dati—no. I was not dating Graham. I wanted to, but he wanted time. And I hadn't heard from him in a month, I corrected myself.

It felt like this was a request for a date, but I could be wrong. Either way, he was nice. Nice to look at or he was trying to be nice and assuage my guilt.

"Bryant?"

"Sorry, Declan, I was looking at my schedule. Yeah, tonight's good."

"You work on the weekends?" I could hear a hint of laughter in his tone.

"Sometimes. I have a court date next week, and it's a challenging one, so I am getting all my homework done," I said.

"That sounds like a good move, but since you already agreed to beers tonight, leave the homework at the office."

"Gladly," I leaned back, stretching. "I'm tired of looking at it, anyway."

"How about The Rye around five?"

"Sounds great," I said. "Although that's a bit more than beer," I added, smiling. I loved The Rye.

"Well, I'm thoughtful like that. I like people to have options. See you later," Declan said.

I hung up, and I could feel the smile on my face. While I had no expectations, he seemed like a good guy. If this was a date, then all the better, but again, I couldn't tell. I hadn't been paying attention after I'd run into him. Well, I had noticed how nice he looked in his workout gear... but the thought of lawsuits drove all that out of my head.

"You're a Higgs," I said to myself.

When Tibby stuck her head in, I was surprised to see that it was after four.

"You want to come out with us tonight?"

I shook my head. "No, thanks. I'm going out for a beer."

Tibby's eyes rose to nearly the ceiling. "Oh?"

"Don't say it like that, you old gossip. I just met someone earlier this week—"

Tibby whooped. "You're back, back in the saddle again," she sang, inviting herself into my office.

"It's not like that! I ran into him out in front and knocked him off his bike."

"Oh, shit. Is this a settlement talk? Why didn't you tell me about this?" She switched from cackling best friend to all law in less than a heartbeat.

"No, it's no big deal. I asked him to let me know that he was all right, because I thought the same thing you did," I grinned at her, "And he told me he was fine, but that I could take him out for a beer for his trouble."

She crossed her arms, looking at me. "Is this a date? Did you really score a date from an accident?"

I was glad in that moment she'd come in. "I don't know. I didn't get that vibe from him, but…" I shrugged. "It feels like a date, even if I'm not sure about him. I feel like a kid!" I threw up my hands. "I've been part of a couple for so long, I don't know whether to scratch my watch or wind my ass!"

Tibby laughed. "Well, if he's interested, he'll let you know. If not, write it off as a business expense."

"You are colder than I am," I stared at her. "How did I miss this when I first asked you to go into business?"

"Blind, like most guys there," she shrugged again. "Underestimating women? Who cares? That's not the point right now. The point is, this could be a date, so you'd better hop to it and pull your shit together."

"What's wrong with my shit?" I looked down at myself.

"God, men." She rolled her eyes. "Go brush your hair,

brush your teeth, and make sure you don't stink. It may not be anything, but that's what you do when it might."

I stopped myself when I remembered that I'd seen her do this countless times. "There's a reason this isn't a guy thing," I said, taking a lofty tone.

"It should be. It's common courtesy. You don't go into court with bad breath. You should go into any meeting the same way."

"I can't believe I'm being lectured by you," I grumbled, getting up to go to the bathroom between our offices.

"You're lucky to have me. Hey, what's this guy's name? What's he do?"

"Why?"

"Because that's what you do, Bryant. You get some info on your friend when they go out with strange people so that if you don't show up on Monday, I have a place to send the police."

"Are you serious?"

She stepped into the bathroom behind me. "Yes. One hundred percent."

I stared at her, but she wasn't budging. "Fine. His name is Declan O'Mara, and I have no idea what he does. He rides a bike for fun," I added.

"That's it? That's all you got?"

"I didn't realize I was supposed to compile a report." I glared.

"All right, if that's the best you can do. Text me when you get home tonight."

"Again, are you for real?"

"I'm your friend." She disappeared back onto her side.

I stared at myself in the mirror. This could be a lot of fuss over nothing.

After a few moments where I peered at my hair in the mirror, Tibby yelled at me again.

"Lock up?"

"You're leaving already?" I called out.

"Yep."

"Slacker."

"Call me and tell me everything. Late tomorrow morning and don't forget to text me tonight!" she added.

"Yes, Mom," I yelled toward her office.

I could hear our staff laughing. They all loved working for us—said it was like working for a brother and sister.

Which was true. Add onto that a good benefits package, and we treated them like part of the family—we didn't have much turnover.

When I finished up, and closed up my office, I headed out to see that our paralegals were leaving.

Darcy, who'd been with us since we'd opened, smiled. "You look good, Bryant."

"Well, good. Have I been looking less than good?"

She exchanged a glance with Tina, our office manager. "You haven't been yourself lately," she said.

Tina nodded.

"That was diplomatic. But true," I sighed. "Sorry if I've been a pain. My head has been up my own ass for too long. However, it's free and clear now, so no more of not-me anymore."

"That's a good thing. It's fine, by the way. Everyone has those months that are terrible," Tina said.

"Have a good weekend," Darcy said.

"You, too, ladies," I smiled.

They left, and I did a walk-through and then locked up.

As the door clicked shut behind me, I found that I was a little nervous.

That I hoped it was a date, and I was scared as hell that it would be. Or that it wouldn't be.

There was no happy medium. As I headed for The Rye Bar, I thought I could solve everything if I just went home and crawled into bed.

Which made me laugh at my own foolishness. It would be what it would be.

But I still hoped it was a date.

y some miracle, I was able to find parking, and got in the door just after five. I scanned the bar which wasn't very big, and saw Declan sitting in one of the leather chairs over by the window. He stood when he saw me.

"Hey," I said as I approached.

He held out his hand. "You can see for yourself," he said as we shook, "That I'm still in one piece and upright."

He was dressed in business casual, with dark khaki pants and a button-up shirt in light blue that made his eyes look even icier. They glowed like beacons.

"That makes my lawyer heart beat a little easier," I said, sitting down across from him.

"Hey! You were supposed to leave the homework at the office," he laughed.

"Trust me, I did."

"I hope so. I took the liberty of ordering you a Manhattan, but you are under no obligation to drink it," he gestured to one of the drinks on the small table.

"Oh, great! Thanks, I love these," I said.

"You've been here?" He picked up his drink and sat back in the chair.

"Yeah, I have a friend who loves this kind of place," I replied, thinking of Xavier.

"These are some of my favorites," he said as he sipped his drink.

I took a drink, and I felt it wash down my throat and into my stomach, where it started to warm me immediately. The Rye was famous for barrel aging their Manhattans. I'd brought Xavier here before and he nearly fell over at how good they were.

Tibby had to drive us home that night, too, I thought.

I was glad she'd badgered me for info tonight, I realized. Now it was time to get a little more.

"Since I was so busy running into you, I didn't ask what you do," I said. I kept it casual. I could feel the work side of me gear up for interrogation, and I didn't want to do that.

He grinned. "I'm a water consultant."

"A what?"

"A water consultant."

"What does that entail?"

DC was always interesting in the many kinds of jobs that brought people here. It was one of the reasons I loved living here. I was glad that Tibby hadn't wanted to move after she got married. I would die here.

"It's a good job for a public service and engineering double major. That was the important point as far as my mother was concerned," he said, still smiling. "You know, put that degree we paid so much for to use, and all that."

I laughed with him. I would have gotten the same response had I gone into any other field than pre-law.

Declan continued, "We look at how to make water more readily available to communities. Not just water, but how to get rid of waste, and all the aspects of water needed for daily life."

"That sounds interesting." I'm not sure whether it is or not, but he's so passionate about it, I find myself interested.

"It is. DC is an old city and figuring out how to upgrade and maintain the water systems here is always a challenge. I've been doing some travel in Europe this year for better ideas. People still have to live, and God knows they'd whine and carry on if too much of life gets disrupted," he rolled his eyes. "So I—" then he stopped. "I'm sorry. I get a little carried away."

"You love your job. That's not a bad thing," I said.

"I really do. I do a lot of work around here on my bike, too, which is good. Except when people run right into me," he grinned.

"Well, you're getting a good drink out of it at least," I said. "Speaking of which, next round is on me. So how long have you been in DC?"

"I just relocated here about four months ago. You?"

"I've been here my whole life."

We talked a little like I remembered you do when you're getting to know someone. I still couldn't tell if this was a date, so after trying to analyze it for the first ten minutes, I gave up.

We'd been there for about an hour when Declan said, "You hungry?"

"What, now you want dinner too?" I asked.

Oh, shit. That was definitely date-like.

He clutched his knee. "Yes. It dulls the pain," and made a face.

"If that will help you on your journey of healing," I said.

We ordered, and before I knew it, it was after ten.

Declan was the first to openly glance at his watch. "I'm

not totally sure that I'm fully healed, although I suppose I can admit I'm on a healing path. But if I don't get to bed, I'll relapse, so I'm going to head out."

"Well, I wouldn't want to see that," I said, feeling shy.

I wasn't sure how to end the evening. I hated this, hated it. Not only the lack of which way to go, or what to do, but the complete lack of control.

"Then you'd better check in with me," Declan said. "I have a ride scheduled tomorrow, but I'm free for dinner tomorrow night." He raised his eyebrows. "On me, this time."

I'd picked up the tab after the first round.

"Okay, that sounds good," I said.

"Give me your cell number," he said, pulling out his phone.

We exchanged numbers, and then he met my eyes. "So it's a date, then."

I opened my mouth, and for a moment, nothing came out. The attraction I'd felt when I first saw him, and then when I saw him tonight rushed in and hit me with the force of a freight train. His eyes were like lasers. They glowed even in this semi-dark bar.

I could feel my entire body respond, and it took me another minute to speak. "Looks that way. I can't let you collapse," I added.

"No, you cannot. Say seven?"

"Sounds good," I managed. His eyes were boring into me, and I could feel all the hormones that had fallen off my radar over the past couple of months come screaming to life. Holy shit, this guy was like live electricity. I'd looked at him while we'd been talking, and nothing like this hit me before.

I wondered if he'd just decided to put his interest out there. If so, I was glad. Every part of me was glad.

He stood and held out a hand. I stood and took it, and the jolt of electricity I'd felt looking into his eyes intensified.

I'd never felt anything like it before. My God.

"Thanks for dinner tonight," he said.

Did he sound breathless? God, I hoped so. I hoped I wasn't the only one.

"It was my pleasure."

"That makes two of us," he said, and his fingers gripped my hand longer than a normal handshake.

"Well, good night," he said, finally letting go of my hand. He took a step, and then stopped, looking back at me. "I'm glad you bumped into me." With a smile, he turned away, and headed out of the bar.

I sat back down, shaken at the strength of my response to him.

This was not the response of someone pining for their lost love, and thinking of Graham, I immediately felt guilty.

The drive home seemed to take longer than normal.

Maybe it was just me.

When I got home to the dark house, I didn't feel like doing anything. I texted Tibby.

I'm home, Mom. Everything's fine.

Thank you. You never know. Tibby sounded like me.

Well now you know I'm safe.

Call me tomorrow.

Will do.

I went to bed. I didn't like the mixed up way I felt, in spite of the intense attraction I felt for Declan. Right now, I was too tired to examine it or beat myself up further. Time for that tomorrow.

*W*hen I got up, the sun was shining, and I stretched in bed, feeling good.

The events of the night before hit me and immediately enveloped me in all the feelings I'd gone to bed to ignore.

I checked the time. Nine a.m. It was too early to call Tibby and ask what the hell this all meant.

I almost called Matt, but decided that while he was pretty chill about me coming out, perhaps he wasn't up for discussing the minutia of dating just yet. Tibby had known forever, and to her, it was no big thing.

Damn it.

I was restless, and rather than sit around and stew, I got up and went for a run.

DC has the reputation of too much traffic, shit parking, and potholes that swallow buses. All of which are true, but Georgetown was something special. I loved running along the canal, and since it was Saturday morning, there weren't the normal crowds you saw during the day.

We grew up close to American University, so this wasn't my childhood neighborhood. But it was my forever home.

I could feel myself calm as I ran along the canal, following my route that took me up one side and back down the other toward home.

Away from Declan, and the fact that his eyes and touch were mesmerizing, I could analyze things. Why was I even looking at the guy? My whole goal was to win back Graham.

Even though he hadn't called.

My thoughts wandered to Graham. Why would he make me wait like this? There was only one answer that kept coming to the forefront, and I didn't like it.

Because he never planned on calling me back.

Or was I being fickle, listening to my body, and my racing hormones?

"Damn it," I muttered, startling the older woman I passed walking her dog.

She muttered something herself, but I'd run past her by the time she got it out. Oh, well. Lots of people talked to themselves. I'd heard such people were the smart ones— crazy, too, but smart.

When I made it back home, I'd come to a decision. I would call Graham. I really enjoyed last night, but I needed to have Graham in a place in my head where things were settled between us. Either we were going to work on it together, or I was going to move on.

I had no illusions, either. Graham had been the man I loved more than anyone else I'd ever dated. Duh. I'd asked him to marry me. No one else before had inspired me to do such a thing.

So while Declan was fantastic, I couldn't hope for more than enjoying time with him. I knew, in the clinical side of my brain, that I needed to process the grief that one of these men would no longer be part of my life.

In spite of where I found myself at the moment, I'd never even allowed myself to think that way.

Wait. I stopped as it hit me.

"Dhameer!" I yelled. "This is some bullshit, man! I need to talk to you!"

My voice echoed through the house. No one answered.

"Shit," I said, kicking off my shoes and heading for the kitchen. I was drinking a glass of water when I heard something, and then a puff of glitter exploded in front of me.

I nearly dropped the glass when I spit through the glitter cloud.

When I finished choking, I looked up to see Dhameer using one of my kitchen towels to pat at himself.

"Hey! That's not going to be permanently glittered, is it?"

"You're worried about the glitter?" He didn't bother to hide the sarcasm.

"Among other things, yes."

"How can I assist you today, Bryant?" His voice was smooth, almost hypnotic.

"You told me I needed to change, and then I would get what I wanted, my dearest wish."

"Yes?" His eyebrows raised and I could tell that he was not sure what I was complaining about, but being polite.

"I changed. I did exactly what Graham wanted, and I told my whole family the truth about me."

"That is excellent. Truth is far more comfortable to live with than deception."

I stared. He was going to make this as difficult as possible.

"So why haven't I gotten what I wanted?"

He sighed, and looked off in the distance for a moment, not speaking. Then he met my eyes, and I was struck by the latent power in his gaze.

"I cannot just make things happen—"

"Bullshit. I know what you did for Tibby, and Xavier told me that you put Olivia in his way, made sure they met," I dismissed the details with a flick of my hand. "So why can't you make this work for me?"

"What did I tell you needed to happen first?"

"That I had to make changes for my dearest wish—"

Now he cut me off. "And you have indeed made changes. You need to consider, however, why you made them, and whether they were the right ones."

"What the…" my voice trailed off. Was he serious?

But Dhameer wasn't done. "You also need to consider what it is you wish for—what you think is your dearest wish? Is that, in fact, your dearest wish? The one close to your heart that you don't often say to yourself? I have set the things in motion that will allow you to realize what it is you wish for—but you must do your part." Now he shrugged. "If you have not, then the things I have put into place for you will not occur."

"You have got to be kidding me. This is your advice? This is even more vague and less of an answer than before!"

"Well, when people get involved in their own lives, in their destiny," a smile sent the side of his mouth up, "Things get confusing, and muddled, and vague."

I muttered something and turned away towards the sink, because I was mad, and I didn't want to look at him.

"You might also want to learn a bit of patience."

I whirled around, ready to tell him to fuck off.

"That's a gift, a freebie, as you say. There's nothing involved in that. Merely advice from one who has been watching humans try to sort themselves for a long time."

"Were you this way with my friends?"

"Tabitha, yes. Xavier angered me, and so I made him forget our conversation, and didn't offer him any help."

Knowing X, this was interesting. Since it took my mind off my problems for a minute, I leaned against the sink and crossed my arms. The sun felt good on my back.

"What did he do to piss you off?"

Dhameer breathed deeply through his nose. "He told me that he was far more observant than I gave him credit for, and that he hadn't found the right woman because he just hadn't seen her. Then he demanded I drop her on him, essentially. Insisting one is intelligent and demanding work from others is not the way to endear oneself."

I burst out laughing. "He's maddening at times, I know. But he's a good guy. Loyal to a fault and does anything for those he loves."

"I watched him with Olivia. You are correct. However, he does not put forth that effort unless it is a very specific group of people. Which is what landed him in the situation he found himself in."

The small smile made an appearance again.

"They are a great couple."

"As are Tabitha and Seth. I would think, Bryant, that you might have a little faith."

"Well, djinn don't do anything for free—there's always a catch. So what am I missing?"

Now he smiled widely, and I could tell he was enjoying himself. "That is for you to discover. I am a djinn, not a road map!" And with a whoosh, and of course, a shower of that damn glitter, he was gone.

"Well, that was just great," I said, going to get my vacuum. "Totally helpful. Thanks, guy!" I yelled at the ceiling. Since he was such a lurker, I'm sure he heard me.

But he didn't answer. What was it he'd said? That people needed to get involved?

"OK," I muttered. "Then I'll be in charge of my own destiny."

11

_F_orty minutes later, I sat on the couch, with my phone on the table in front of me. I had picked up the phone to dial Graham seventy-gazillion times and always chickened out before I hit the green 'Call' button.

Why was this so hard?

Fuck it. I needed to make this happen. I needed to be in charge. Without thinking, I hit his contact info, and then the green button, and held the phone to my ear, not giving myself time to hang up again.

One ring.

Two.

Three.

"Hello?"

"Hey, it's me," I said.

"Oh, hey, Bryant," Graham said.

Why was he sounding surprised at all? Was I off his contact list?

I didn't let myself get distracted. I was on a mission.

"How are you? I haven't heard from you in a while," I said.

I could hear someone—the TV, maybe—in the background.

There was a muffled sound as Graham said something away from the phone, and then he came back.

Someone, then.

"Yes, I know. I told you I needed time."

"I think that a heads up would have been nice," I said. Easy, I told myself.

"Well, you're right. I haven't wanted to call, but I'm glad you did," Graham said.

He was so blunt and honest. Even when it was uncomfortable, it was one of the things I appreciated and loved about him.

"Why is that?" I asked.

The noises in the background faded as though he'd walked into another room. I wondered, again, because I'd lost track of how many times I'd wondered this, where he was staying. And with whom.

"Because I have been thinking about us, a lot. Even though I haven't shared that with you, I haven't been ignoring your request."

I couldn't tell where this was going. "I'm glad you have," I said. "Have you come to any decisions?"

He sighed. "Yes, I have. I love you, and part of me will always love you. I can't marry you, though."

"Why not? You said yes before!" Now I was angry.

"Because I thought you'd finally seen the light." Graham was no slouch in the taking up for himself department, and he fired back at me. "You didn't see the light, Bry. You let me, once again, shine the light on you, and on us, and then lead you, practically by the hand, to the way to get through it all. You don't do any of the emotional work on your own. I have to do it all. If we married, it would be the same as it's always been. Me nagging, you finally giving in, and then expecting to be the hero for succumbing to the nagging spouse."

He stopped and took a breath. When he spoke again, he was calmer.

"I don't want that. I don't want that for you, and I sure as hell don't want that for me. Whatever is going on with you, I deserve better. And that's the direction I'm heading now."

"You had this all lined up," I said before I could stop myself.

"Does it matter?" He was cool.

Which meant I was right.

"No, you're right. It doesn't matter. I'm sorry to have bothered you, but I'm glad this is out in the open," I retreated to my professional mien.

"I'm glad you called. I wasn't comfortable with this hanging around, and I... well, I hadn't worked up the courage to call you."

My heart nearly broke. This was the Graham I knew, the one I loved.

"I understand," I said quietly. I was afraid to say more. I might burst into tears.

There was a noise in the background again, a voice. One voice.

I heard Graham whisper something.

But not to me.

"Listen, this is awkward as hell, and I am really sorry. But I'm glad you called. I have always been honest with you."

"Thank you. I won't call again," I said.

"Okay. But you can call if you want. Take care of yourself, Bry."

As he put down the phone, I could hear the voice more clearly, and it was a man's voice.

I hit the red button, letting the phone fall to the couch, and letting the tears finally come.

I lay awake all night, replaying the conversation in my head.

He'd dumped me by phone. Using my nickname, like we were still... something. With another guy hanging around, like a fly near the flypaper.

It was over.

It was totally, completely over.

What the hell had happened?

he damned sun hurt when it hit my eyes. That must be the result of all the salt water. My head hurt, and the ringing phone wasn't helping.

I scrabbled around for my phone and answered it without looking to see who was calling. "Yes?"

"Bryant! Are you dead? Because if not, you need to tell me what is going on! I've been calling you all morning!" Tibby was pissed.

I glanced at the clock. Holy shit. It was after ten in the morning.

"I am sorry, Tib. Fuck, I didn't realize it was so late. I'm getting up now," I tossed the bedclothes aside, feeling the adrenaline rush through me.

"No, wait!" She almost yelled. "Stop and tell me what's going on. It's Sunday, goofball. You're not late for anything. I'm just not used to you not answering. I wanted to hear what happened on Friday. Somehow, you forgot to update me!"

"Oh, Christ," I said. The enormity of what had

happened yesterday hit me again. Just when I'd managed to put it out of the front of my thoughts.

"Forget it." Tibby changed tack. "You sound horrible. I'm grabbing stuff for bloody Marys and I'll be there soon. By myself," she added. "Do you have food I can cook?"

"I guess," I said. Why did it matter?

"Never mind. I'll be there in an hour. An hour-ish," she added. "I'll grab some food."

"Okay," I said.

"Hey, Bry?"

Hearing my nickname made the tears leak again.

"I love you," she said, and then she hung up.

I crawled back into bed. Tibby had a key.

I didn't hear her knock, or even come in. But I felt someone shaking my foot, and when I opened my eyes again, the shade had been lowered, and Tibby stood next to the bed.

"Get up. I have a bloody Mary with your name on it, and some toast, and if you want it, eggs and potatoes."

Food sounded both great and horrible. Tibby didn't wait for an answer, sailing out of the room.

For once, I was glad she was so bossy.

When I made it down to the kitchen, she shoved a coffee cup, as well as a glass filled with a bloody Mary, at me.

"Sit," she commanded. "And once you've had a few sips, tell me what you want that won't make you throw up."

"I love you," I said.

"I know," her back was to me as she spooned potatoes off the stove. "I love you, too. Spill."

Sighing, I wondered where to start.

"I called Graham last night," I said.

"He hasn't called you since you guys talked?" Her back was still to me, her tone noncommittal and light.

"No. I went for a run and decided that after a month, I deserved to hear something. I mean, there's a proposal sitting there, waiting for a response. Well," I amended, "There was."

"Go on," Tibby turned and leaned against the island, eating. Her face was carefully neutral.

Normally I'd be annoyed she was using work face on me, but today, I was glad. It made it easier without her comments as my best friend.

"I called him. I mean, for God's sake. He hadn't called me in a month! And he said, when I did talk with him, that he had been avoiding it."

The weight of all that Graham had said hit me, and I dropped my head. I didn't want Tib to see me fall apart.

"What else did he say?" Her voice was quiet.

Without looking up, I replied, "That he felt he did all the work for the emotional side of things in our relationship, and that if we got back together, he'd still be doing it. He said that I only moved forward because he forced my hand."

At that point, I ventured a glance at her. "What?" I could see that she wanted to say something, but was holding back.

"How honest do you want me to be?"

"Honest, but can you go gentle? I'm already feeling like shit."

Tibby nodded. She knew what I meant. "Listen, Bry, I liked Graham. But he always went on about how much he did, and how you never did enough. I know there's give and take in every relationship, but he made it all one way for him, and all the other, less-than great way for you."

"That's what you say about someone you like?"

"No, that's what I say to my BFF who is hurting from

being rejected by someone who wasn't ever good enough for him." Her tone brooked no argument.

"How can you say that?" I asked.

She inhaled and crossed her arms. "How far do you want this to go?"

"What else is there, Tib?" I was suspicious now.

"When you told me what happened, how he had a bag packed, even though he'd said yes, I… Well," she looked away, and looked uncomfortable.

"You what?"

"I had him followed," Tibby got out in a rush.

"You what?" I asked slowly, not sure I'd heard right.

"I had him followed. Even had my guy sit close to him and his friend when they were out a couple of times. He was seeing the guy, or had something going with him before he moved out, Bry. He wasn't being honest with you, for all that shit he spouts."

"You really do hate him, don't you?" I asked.

"Right now? Yes, I do. You're tying yourself into a damn knot because you are trying to be something he says you need to, and he's been lying to you. The whole time he's been stringing you along!" Her hesitation was gone, and now she was mad.

I wanted to yell at her, tell her that her bossy britches shit had just gone too far—but I knew it hadn't. I was the guy who had told her I got to vet her dates. And she'd let me. We looked out for one another.

"When did you have him followed?" I found that asking made me feel tired, and about a hundred years old.

"Not until after he moved out. He's living with the guy," she added.

"Why didn't you tell me?"

Tibby shrugged. "Why, if you weren't going to get back together? I thought you going out with that other guy—the one you still haven't told me much about—meant that you were starting to move on."

"He's really with someone else?"

"They hold hands in public. Maybe they're not together, but that's not the vibe the PI got."

I laid my head down on the counter. "I loved—love him," I said to the cool granite.

"I know," Tibby said. "I'm sorry."

"Why did he even say yes?" I turned my head so I could kind of see her.

"I don't know? He got mean? He was being a shit that day? I don't know. Did he really tell you he didn't want to do the heavy lifting anymore?"

"Yes."

"Asshole," she said. "I know this hurts. But he was tossing shit up at you to cover his own bullshit."

"Seems like it, doesn't it?" I spoke to the granite again. "Fuck. Tib, this may take a while to…" I couldn't say the words. Couldn't say *get over him*. I just couldn't.

"You know, this means there is something else?"

"What are you talking about?"

"Dhameer. What he said to you."

I gave her the one-eyed stink eye. "Why the hell are you talking about him? My life just fell apart here."

"I know, but eventually, you have to come back to life. And you have a djinn who somehow set something up in your favor. He's not a jerk. Nothing is free with Dhameer, but he doesn't set you up to get hurt."

"Oh, no?" I asked, the bitterness seeping out and burning an acidic hole in the granite countertop.

"No, he doesn't. Maybe it means…" Tibby stopped. Took a deep breath. "Maybe it means that your heart's desire is in a bit of a different direction."

I laughed. I couldn't help it. "Could you dance around

that one some more, please?" I pushed my body up off the island to look at her.

"I could, but I thought I was pretty much at the bottom of the barrel as it was," Tibby said.

"I can't think about that right now, Tib," I got serious again. "I've just lost everything I ever wanted."

Her mouth opened and then closed. Good. I wasn't in the mood for platitudes of any sort.

"OK. Then how about we drink these bloody Marys and make it so I have to call a cab?"

"OK. But you're cooking and cleaning."

She laughed, and it was a testament to our friendship that she didn't bitch about doing everything. She stayed with me all afternoon, and we didn't mention Graham again.

"You going to be OK?" She asked as she got ready to leave.

I was impressed that her phone hadn't gone off at all— she must have told Seth it was a no fly zone today.

"Not yet, but I guess I'll live."

"Listen, tell your family that there's no engagement," Tibby looked serious. "Otherwise it will come up when you really don't want it to."

"What, you're the expert on this?"

"No, just the expert on all the awkward family shit."

"OK, I'll call my mom tomorrow. She'll spread the news and make it a little easier."

"It's OK to call her, Bryant. That's what moms are there for."

"Thanks for coming over, Tib."

She gave me a big hug and kissed my cheek. "I love you, jackass. I'm always here for you. You have an open invite for any time you need to swing by, OK? I mean it. *We* mean it," she added.

"Go home. Your guy's been pretty patient all day. I'll let you know if I need propping up."

"OK. See you tomorrow."

"Night."

I closed the door behind her. I was exhausted.

As I fell into bed, I thought, Why, Graham? The vision of him getting into the car with the other guy was never going to leave.

Damn it.

I finished cleaning up the kitchen and headed back to bed. There was nothing to do but to keep putting one foot in front of the other and hope that time would help me move forward and away from what I thought my future would be.

I looked at the phone. I might as well call my mom tonight. It wasn't too late. Get it over with now and then be done with it.

She answered on the second ring. "Bryant! Sweetheart, how are you?"

"Actually Mom, not so good."

And for the second time this year, I got to tell my mom that no wedding was in my future. I think it sucked even more this time.

I didn't think that I could feel worse, but hearing my mom tell me she was so sorry, and hear the hint of tears in her voice made me feel guilty.

Which made no sense, but there it was, and I couldn't tell her anything other than it would be all right, eventually.

I tried really hard to believe it.

13

When I woke up Monday morning, my eyes didn't feel like sandpaper.

So that was a point on the plus side.

But I sure didn't want to go to work. I knew myself, however. If I sat at home, I'd stew over what I should have said, could I have done anything differently, and on and on.

When in reality, if what Tibby told me was true—and I didn't have any reason to doubt her, other than I didn't want to accept it—then there was nothing I could have done to change the way things ended.

Graham was on his way out. He'd been on his way out. Why hadn't I seen it? We'd lived together.

I had no idea. Honestly, I didn't know how I'd missed it, but I had. If I were being honest, and today I was, I did have a slight question in my head, remembering seeing Graham get into the car when he walked out that night.

But I'd ignored it and shoved it aside. Because who wants to think the worst of someone they love? Particularly if thinking the worst means you were a patsy, and someone fooled you.

No one likes looking like a fool.

I sighed and took myself to work.

Tibby was already there as were the ladies in the office. Everyone said hi but kept it low-key. Tib must have warned them.

Normally, I'd be pissed, but today, I appreciated it. Not like I hadn't done something similar for her, back when she was dealing with her men troubles.

However, as I made myself turn my mind to work, I realized that I would also have to stop thinking of an end goal with Graham as part of it.

That pierced through my heart like a sword.

Nope. Not now. I shoved those thoughts aside. I wasn't ready to deal with that. Work would have to do for the moment.

Thank God for work.

I could tell that I was on edge. I took Tibby with me to the court appearance we'd talked before my whole world fell sideways, and as she predicted, the guy on the other side nearly blew a gasket when he saw her.

"What's his deal?" I whispered as we settled in on our side.

She shrugged. "He asked me out once. He's been pissed ever since I politely declined. Feels sure I'm not right. Never misses a chance to throw shade either." She grinned at me. "So I enjoy seeing him fall on his ass."

And fall on his ass he did. Tibby was right. It was good to see.

The hearing was the only bright spot in my entire

week. I felt like I held a tiny Band-Aid on a gaping flesh wound.

It had to get better, right?

———

A week later, and the cut the sword made through my heart was still there. Even though I felt that some sort of healing had begun, overall, I was achy and sore.

So when the phone rang, late Monday night, when I was trying to get this shit done so I could go home, I was abrupt when I answered.

"Higgs," I said, letting the phone rest on my shoulder.

"Hey, Bryant, it's Declan."

A moment, and then, "Oh. Hey, Declan. Hang on," I set the phone down, and physically put the paperwork away from me.

I felt bad. I'd been so busy distracting myself, I hadn't thought of Declan much. Was I supposed to call him? I couldn't remember. Too busy wallowing in my own self-pity was more like it, but I felt I could give myself a week or so.

The week is up, my snide inner critic reminded me.

Shut up, I shot back.

I picked up the phone. "How are you? Sorry it took me a minute—I wanted to get the papers out of my line of sight."

He laughed, and I smiled. I'd forgotten how warm his laugh was. "I get it. I've been practically underwater all week."

Now I laughed. "Under water? Isn't that an occupational hazard?" It felt weird to laugh, to smile. I hadn't done much the last seven days.

"Yeah, it can be. But we heard back from the DC folks, so the flurry of emails is like trying to walk a straight line in a snow storm. I'm finally back to familiar ground, but it took all week."

"I get that. It's like that here, when clients all go off the deep end at the same time."

"I didn't want you to think I was ignoring you," he said. "I know I said we'd have dinner last week, and then I didn't call. I hate to admit it, but I sometimes work on the weekend, too."

Oh, God. Another upfront, honest one. The ache in my heart hit me hard.

"I didn't think that," I said, not really sure what to say.

There was silence on the other end.

"Is everything okay?" Declan asked.

"What do you mean?" Did I sound that bad?

"You don't sound like yourself, at least the way I've interacted with you. Is this a bad time?"

Now it was my turn to be silent.

He spoke again. "Listen, I like you, and I'd like to get to know you better. But if it's not a great time, let me know."

I sighed. "It's not a great time, and that has nothing to do with you."

"Is this work or personal?"

"More personal."

"You want to talk about it?"

I thought about it. "Do you really want to hear it? Other people's sad stories are just not that interesting, generally, outside of those involved."

He actually chuckled. "I don't mind other people's stories, sad or otherwise. I'm serious in that I want to get to know you. So if you feel up to it, tell me about it."

Did I want to do this? He was new, an unknown. It had been Graham and me for so long.

Well, he said he wanted to know. "I ended a long-term relationship—" I stopped. Holy shit. "A couple of months ago."

"That's tough. It takes time to move past it."

I sighed. Again. "Yeah, it does. I wasn't the one who ended it. I wanted to move things to something more, and he…" The pain washed over me. "He said he did, too. But when it came to it, he left."

"That really sucks, Bryant. I'm sorry."

"Me, too. It wouldn't be so bad, but things weren't…" I hesitated, looking for the right word. "There wasn't closure. He left a lot of things hanging, and when I pressed for some kind of answer, one way or the other, he told me that it had been over for him. It would have been nice had he shared that," I finished, the bitterness seeping out a little.

"Sounds kind of selfish," Declan said.

"It was. I've learned some more things that were going on that I wasn't initially aware of, and yes, it makes all this even more selfish. So without getting all caught up in my drama, I think it's important that you're aware of that. I like you, too. But I'm not in the best place." I felt I needed to be honest.

"Thanks for being honest with me. I think you can put up with a lot if there is honesty between people. I'm sorry it's been such a rough time. I don't like relationships that end but drag on at the same time. It's brutal."

"That's exactly what it is," I said. It felt good to talk about this with someone who didn't know all the gory details, and could see it from a slightly different point of view.

"Well, in the spirit of honesty, I still would like to see

you. It doesn't have to be anything major, or intense. It may not be anything. But I like you, and I'd like to spend time with you. No pressure."

"No pressure?" I asked. "No promises, either."

"Well, one promise," he said.

"Which is?"

"Don't stop being honest. It's always worse to learn that someone's blowing smoke at you."

"I agree," I said.

"Now that we've settled that, let's talk about something more pleasant. How about happy hour somewhere on Friday?"

"That sounds good," I said.

"Are you just trying to flatter me?" He asked, and I could hear the laughter in his voice.

"No. It does sound good. I'm tired of myself, moping around."

"I find that you can only feel sorry for yourself for so long, and then you have to kick your own ass," he said.

"I think I'm almost there—the kicking your own ass part," I added.

"Well, good. Let's get together at the end of the week and see if you're there."

"Sounds good," I said.

"I'll text you, then?"

"Yes."

"Great. Thanks for being honest, Bryant. I appreciate it," he said.

"Oh, well, ah, you're welcome?"

"See you later. I'll text you."

"Okay."

"Night."

"Night," I said as he ended the call.

That was unexpected. I hadn't thought about him at all, but talking with him made me feel better.

I didn't want to use him or have him be a rebound. I'd seen that with some of my friends, and I thought it was mean.

Again, though, what the hell did I know? I'd been out of the dating world forever.

However, I decided that if I kept being honest with myself, I'd be able to do that for Declan, too. That way, this wouldn't end in some massive drama-laden cluster.

I pulled the paperwork back in front of me. I still needed to get through this crap. There was plenty of time to over think the Declan situation.

---

*A*s it turned out, there wasn't a lot of time to over think anything. Tuesday morning right after I got in, my mother called.

"Hello, darling," she said when I picked up.

"What's going on, Mom?"

"I wanted to know if you were free tomorrow night. I know it's last minute, but things have been a bit up in the air," she added.

That didn't make a lot of sense, but if I spent time trying to figure out everything my mom said, I'd be forever occupied.

"Um, yeah, I think so." I checked my calendar. "Yes, I'm free. At the house?"

"Yes, around six? Do you have anything pressing at the office tomorrow?"

"No, I can get out of here at a decent hour."

"Good, sweetheart. I'd like to see you. I've been thinking about you since we spoke last week."

What had we talked about?

Oh. That's right. The whole 'forget my engagement'.

Great.

"Thanks, mom." I wasn't sure where she was going with this.

"I'm sorry I wasn't there for you more," she said, and I could hear the emotion in her voice.

"Oh, Mom, no. Don't do that. I didn't want anything from anyone. I'm not good around other people when I'm miserable. You know that."

"You're so rarely miserable that it's easy to forget you can be too," she said.

Her words hit me with the weight of a sledgehammer. She was right. I put a lot of effort into keeping things in my life on an even keel.

I'd done it when Tib and I went into business. I loved her, but she was a whole lot of drama. I set boundaries so that her drama didn't take over her life and fuck up our business.

I'd done it with Graham, too. In spite of everything he supposedly had done, I managed things with him, too.

Keep everything on an even keel, keep everything ticking along. Everything's great here, nothing to see! Move alone, we're all good here.

Jesus.

It was too much to think about all at once.

Plus, Mom was still on the phone.

"Bryant? Are you still there?"

"Yeah, I am. Sorry, Mom. I'm just swamped at work, but I'll be there tomorrow. And don't worry about the other stuff, Mom. I'm working through it. It's just not any kind of fun right now," I added.

Normally, I didn't let my mom in on that much.

"It never is, when you're disappointed that someone

else doesn't share the same vision. I'm sorry we haven't been available for you, but I am now. We both are."

Despite her fumbling, I appreciated what she was trying to say. "Thanks, Mom. I'm going to be okay. I'm just feeling a little kicked around, that's all."

"Well, we're looking forward to seeing you. It's the family," she added.

"Okay. See you tomorrow."

"I love you, Bryant."

"Love you too, Mom."

After the call was done, I looked at the phone. It almost sounded like my mom was feeling really guilty—I wasn't sure why. It's not like I told her all about Graham and our life together.

She didn't have anything to feel guilty for.

14

$\mathcal{J}$t turned out I was wrong about my mom's guilt, too.

I was having quite a month. Good thing I didn't gamble. Because I'd have lost my ass in the past month.

Although things started out just fine.

When I got to my parents' place, I was in a good mood. Traffic hadn't been terrible, and I was looking forward to seeing them, and my brothers. Maybe the kids would be there, and that would be nice, too.

It felt like I was coming up for air after being stuck somewhere that it was hard to breathe. Everything smelled fresh, and new.

Which was nice.

My mom answered the door and pulled me into a hug. "How are you, darling?"

"I'm okay, Mom. I told you. It's getting better."

"Well, good. Come in, let's get you a drink."

She shooed me in toward the drawing room—I couldn't believe she called it that, but we did in fact have a drawing room. Once inside, I found my dad and Granddad, Matt and Priscilla, and Casey. Melissa wasn't around. Nor, were it seemed, the kids.

Which made me sad. It was good for kids to see people of diverse lives get together. But apparently, not everyone thought so.

"No Melissa?" I asked Casey quietly as we made our way to the dining room.

He shook his head, but didn't say anything.

Seeing him, I not only felt sad, but angry. I was the same person I'd been before, but she didn't seem to see it that way.

I couldn't do anything about it. I felt bad for Casey, and sorry that my life was causing him friction, even though Melissa's feelings were her own to manage. It didn't mean that I wasn't unhappy for my brother.

As my mom and dad brought out the food, conversation was idle, but I picked up on a thread of… something. I couldn't tell what it was, but there was an undercurrent.

What was this fresh hell?

Then I laughed at myself. *It's not all about you, Bryant*, I thought.

Once everyone was eating, my mom cleared her throat. "Thank you to everyone who was able to make it to dinner tonight. I know it was a last minute get together, but Dad and I really appreciate it." She smiled.

"I asked everyone to dinner because I'm really concerned about what appears to be a growing rift in this family and I wanted to see how we can work together to help heal it."

Was she talking about me? About Melissa's reaction to me?

Casey must have had the same thought, because he said, "Mom, I don't know if there's anything we can do, if you're referring to Melissa."

"I am, dear. I don't appreciate that Melissa is insisting on keeping the children away. They are part of this family whether she wants to be or not."

"I can't tell my wife that my kids have to do something she disapproves of," Casey started.

"Is this because of me?" I put down my fork. "What is she not allowing the kids to do?"

Casey flushed. "She won't let them come to anything you're going to be at."

Wow. Just… wow. That hurt, and the sword that Graham had driven into my heart came back and stabbed me again. I put my hand on my chest as it was a physical pain.

"She expects me to not show up for family events anymore?" My voice came out in a whisper.

A moment of hesitation, and then Casey nodded.

The rest of the table was silent.

"Did you all know about this?" I asked.

Slowly, everyone nodded.

"So what is it you're asking me?" I could hear the steel in my voice. My heart may be bleeding, but to hell with this, if it was what I thought it was.

"We're not asking you to do anything," Mom said. "This isn't on you. It doesn't change the fact, however, that this means things will be bumpy for a bit. I guess we are asking something—for you to be patient."

"Why is it I need to be patient with the narrow, close-minded thoughts of someone else? Her attitudes are not my problem! I've always been respectful of everyone in this family. Melissa needs to learn how to do the same!" I could feel my anger rising.

"No, they are not, but they do affect us all. Including you," Mom said. "Don't you miss the kids?"

I stopped. "Yeah, I do. So what, you want me to stop

showing up? Because that won't change things for me. And you'll be making me change for someone else's wrong. Sorry, Case, but she's wrong," I looked at my brother.

"I know that, and you know that—we all know that," he sounded frustrated. "I've been hearing about it daily, and I'm really tired of it."

"I'm sorry," I said, and I meant it. "I don't know what to say, and I'm feeling kind of ambushed here. Like, I don't know what you expect me to do, and I feel like you're asking me to do something. This isn't my problem to fix. I can't fix it!"

"No, you can't. I have to say, I'm pretty disappointed that she's taking this point of view," Mom said.

"Dad, what do you think?" Matt interjected.

"I understand her surprise, but Bryant isn't any different from the guy he was before he told us," Dad said, frowning. "It was a shock to me, and I needed some time—"

"You honestly had no idea?" Priscilla asked.

"You did?" I interjected.

"We always knew. Matt won the bet, remember?" She smiled.

"I did," Matt looked smug.

I remembered that he and Casey had a bet, but I hadn't thought it was a big deal.

Casey rolled his eyes. "For the record, I wasn't shocked. I don't care. As long as you're not an asshole,"

"Casey! Language!" Mom got her oar in.

"And as long as the person you're with isn't either, what the hell do I care who you date?"

"Did Melissa know about the bet?" I asked.

Casey shook his head. "It wasn't that big of a deal. But after dinner the last time, she went on and on. I'm really sorry, man. I didn't know she felt this strongly about it."

"So what, I can't see my niece and nephew? Is she afraid the gay will somehow rub off?"

"I don't know. She's pretty pissed at me right now," Casey shrugged.

"This is not your problem, Bryant," Priscilla leaned in. "It's one hundred percent on Melissa."

"That's all well and good," I said, "But Casey would probably like to stay married. And I would like to see Casey Jr and Hannah again before they're adults."

"So what would you suggest?" Dad asked.

"Why is everyone asking me? I'm not going to change for Melissa. She's being a bigot, and her thought process is pretty outdated. I've been around those kids since they were babies and there's never been any problem. She had no issues with me babysitting when it worked out for her," I added.

"All I am asking is that we all have a little patience and give one another a little extra space. Nothing has to be done. Although, Casey, I think you ought to tell Melissa that as their father, you can bring them to a family dinner."

"Mom," Casey said.

His tone indicated this wasn't the first time she'd mentioned this to him.

Mom held up her hands. "I'm not interfering. I don't interfere in my children's concerns. But I am capable of offering a suggesting without being a meddling old biddy."

A moment of silence hung in the air, and then the entire table burst into laughter. My mom's suggestions were legendary, and we'd all been on the receiving end.

"Well, call me names if you like. But I don't care for talking about one of my children without them knowing. And if we can end this conversation in laughter, with everyone aware, I'm fine, and I'll keep my peace." She glanced at me as she spoke, and I saw why she'd been feeling guilty. My mom didn't get involved in taking sides, or talking behind the backs of any of us. She never had.

I smiled back at her, grateful that she'd dragged this out into the open. Her words brought more laughter and with that, conversation returned to lighter topics. I was feeling better because I wasn't being booted from the family homestead. I figured I had to get through another half-hour, and then this particularly embarrassing dining experience would be over.

"Hey, Bryant," Priscilla said. She stopped, a look of hesitation on her face.

"Yeah?"

"What happened with Graham?"

So much for the easy half-hour to escape.

I sighed. "Do you really want to hear my tale of woe?"

All five of them nodded their heads.

"I asked him to marry me. He said no, and he left."

"That night?" Matt asked.

"He had a bag packed, and a car waiting."

"Why did he say yes?" Mom looked confused.

"I don't know. Well, I think I do now," I added.

"What do you mean? Don't speak in riddles," my dad grumbled.

I sighed again. This was so humiliating to admit. "Tibby had him followed—"

Matt and Casey hooted with laughter.

"Yeah, I know, but I love her for that. Anyway, she had him followed, and he moved out with another guy. So she had our PI loiter near him and this other guy, and he overheard them talking. Apparently, Graham was seeing him before he moved out." I looked down. I didn't want to cry, not even in front of my family.

"What a bastard," Priscilla said.

I looked up. "Yes, he is. But I didn't know that, and last

week, I called him. Right after I told you guys the truth, I told him that I'd come out. It was always one of the problems between us. I asked him to come back, so we could start again. He said no that he needed some time. A month went by, and I felt like I deserved to hear something, so last week, I called him."

Now I felt anger sliding through me. "He said no for good this time, because, and this was his reason, he did all the emotional heavy lifting in our relationship, and if he came back, it would be the same thing, and he deserved better."

"God, what a nasty thing to say," Priscilla said. "Talk about deflection! I know this must really hurt, but you dodged a bullet with that one."

Matt nodded. "Yeah, he hasn't even had the guts to tell you there's someone else? That's crappy."

My family heaped condemnation on Graham's head. I hoped that wherever he was, his ears were on fire, and he couldn't figure out why.

For the first time since this whole thing had blown up in my face, I felt a little better. Yes, my sister-in-law was looking like she had a raging bigot closeted inside her. Yes, I'd been dumped not once, but twice by the guy I thought was the love of my life.

But my family supported me, and I loved hearing them give me their opinions.

I'd been going over all the things that Graham had said to me and seeing where I'd made mistakes. I'd been so busy faulting myself that I hadn't taken the time to see why he might be more than willing to lay blame at my feet.

To make himself feel better about his actions.

I'd get through this. With my friends, and my family, there was no way I wouldn't.

I left dinner to hugs and feeling better than I'd felt in months.

I was going to do my level best to stop thinking about him. He was in the past, and while I couldn't turn off love like a faucet, I could start cutting down the water flow.

Water.

That made me think of Declan.

I still had a happy hour date with him on Friday.

I'd made the date with him because I couldn't find a reason to say no, not when he was being so decent about my whole mess.

Now I found myself looking forward to it.

---

*W*hen I got into work the next day, I gave Tibby the brief overview of my family dinner while we were fixing our coffee.

She was furious with Melissa. "My God, what century does she live in?"

"Not the one the rest of us do, apparently. I can understand her problems with my lifestyle, even if I think she's ridiculous," I put lifestyle in air quotes. "But to act like I have a disease, you know, *the gay*, and that it might land on the kids is just ridiculous."

"At least everyone else is supportive."

I nodded. "It doesn't make her any less shitty, but it makes me feel a little better to know that she's standing alone with her thoughts on this."

Tibby frowned. "Like it's her business, anyway. This is no worse than if you had a crazy girlfriend."

"You would know, huh?"

"Shut up. I was very good after we made our agreement. You hated him, he was gone."

"True. But look what problems crazy caused for you."

"Are you siding with Melissa?" Tibby's eyebrows rose.

"No, but I do understand not wanting crazy in your close circle."

"Well, even though Graham is a shit, he's not crazy. And you're certainly not. She was happy to use you to babysit," she added.

I shrugged. It was funny that she went to the same place I did regarding me watching the kids. "Maybe, maybe not. All the things he did to make me feel horrible, all while cheating his sanctimonious ass off…" I trailed off. Despite my intentions, I'd thought about Graham after I got home last night, and I'd woken up mad at him.

It was the first time I'd been anything other than angry at myself or sad that he was gone. I saw it as improvement.

"There's that. Okay, since we have you momentarily sorted, can we get back to work?"

I leaned around Tibby and looked out the window into the small courtyard in the back of our office building. "Holy shit, did you see that?"

She turned. "See what?"

"The snow."

Tibby looked at me as though I'd suggested walking through the office naked. "What is in your coffee this morning, Bry?"

"Nothing. But you're nagging me to get to work, rather than loaf in the break room. Hell has frozen over and it's snowing on a summer day."

Her mouth fell open, and she chucked her napkin at me. "Jerk."

"Well, it is a first," I said, laughing as I made it to the door. "Maybe I should go and play the lottery, too."

"Just for that, I'm not coming with you today. You go

and battle that old dragon," she sniffed, and turned her back to me to finish up her coffee.

"Oh, please," I said as I left. "You can't resist the challenge."

She said a rude word loudly as I closed my office door behind me.

Tibby did come with me to the afternoon meeting because she couldn't resist the challenge and she didn't care for the attorney we were working with.

She pretty much wiped the floor with the woman, although it was done in a polite, genteel fashion. I loved to watch her work. Even after all this time, people still under-estimated her.

And then it was Friday.

I chose my clothes with a little more care, fussing over my hair. It wasn't necessary—we kept everything we needed at the office—but it calmed my nerves to go through the rituals.

Even though I'd already been out on my first date with Declan, in my head, it hadn't been a first date. It was just a nice time out with a nice guy.

For me, it had moved to date territory.

I brushed my hair over once more and then looked into the mirror. "That's what it's going to be."

For a Friday, we were swamped at work. I don't know what it is, maybe our clients all have some secret email chain or something, but they all went off the deep end in one form or another today. Our billable hours went up, but Tib and I were hopping all day.

After lunch, Declan texted me.

Hey, how about Maxime? Happy hour mussels!
That sounds great, I responded.
See you at 6
OK

I waited to see if he was going to text back, but since he didn't, I got back to my pile of distress work.

At 5:30, I stepped into her office, and collapsed in a chair. "What the hell? Everyone needed their hands held today!"

"It's that potential legislation. It's got everyone looking over their bits and having lots of time to think. You earned your keep today, pretty boy," Tibby laughed. "What's on your agenda tonight?"

My cheeks got hot, and I hesitated before answering. Tibby, of course, saw it.

"What? What do you have going on to look like that?"

"I have a date," I said.

"With bike guy? Devlan? What's his name?"

"With Declan, yes."

Her smile faded as she peered at me. "Does he know your whole deal?"

"When you say it like that, it sounds so Jerry Springer."

"Oh, stop. You know I wasn't inferring that. I just wondered how honest you've been with him."

"Are you giving me shit?"

"I might be. You're not exactly in the baggage-free territory, Bryant."

"Says the queen of baggage."

"Hey, my baggage is now on one small cart, and it's a cart I share with my darling, devoted husband, so you can step off my baggage."

I had to laugh. "You're right. Seth is a brave man."

"No, just a smart one," she said with an infuriating amount of smugness. "And I was totally honest with him after we met again."

"Come on. I've been out with this guy once. I'm not going to dump my whole sad tale on him right now. That's a sure way to not have another date with him."

"Are you ready to date?"

"I don't know, honestly. When I told him, he said let's take it slow, be friends, and see what happens."

"Really?" She sat back in her chair, folding her hands in her lap. "That's pretty impressive." She looked over my head in what I called her 'thinking' look. Then she looked back at me. "All right. You can date him."

"Hey, you don't get to vet my dates."

"I do now. You're not in the best place, thanks to that asshole Graham."

I was about to tell her to piss off, when I realized that she was just trying to help, trying to do for me what I'd done for her so long ago.

"All right, Mom. You can give your opinion, and I won't be rude when you do."

"If it goes to five dates, you have to have dinner with me and Seth."

"I'll see about it," I said. "You can't tell me what to do."

She laughed as she got up. "Yes, I can. Friend prerogative. But I won't tell you what to do for another four dates. Call me tomorrow and gossip? Where are you going, by the way?"

"I suppose. And we're meeting at Maxime."

"You'd better call. Maxime will be nice. All righty, then. Night, Bry. Have a good time."

"You too, old married lady."

She didn't rise to the bait, only laughed.

I heard the door close as she left and then I ran to the bathroom to look at my hair one more time.

15

I stopped as I walked along the sidewalk toward the restaurant. My stomach was in knots, and I felt my palms sweating. The nerves were back in full force.

"Stop it," I muttered to myself. It wasn't like I hadn't met this guy before.

But before, I wasn't interested in him. Well, I was. But I wasn't focused on him. I was going out with him because it seemed nice, and I was focused on… I wouldn't say his name. We were done. Done. Remember that.

I needed to remember not to go on about he-who-will-not-be-mentioned-by-me either.

A hostess swung the door open. I scanned the room and saw Declan sitting at a table toward the back. He waved, and I headed for him.

"Hey, you're right on time," he said. "You must have pleased the parking Gods."

I laughed. I loved where I lived and worked, but parking was hell. It was an accepted thing, but that didn't make it any less hellish.

"Something like that," I said. "How are you?"

He looked fantastic. His eyes were so blue, so vibrant, even in the slightly darkened room.

"Ready to not go into work again," he grimaced. "Or at least, not talk to a DC employee again."

I sat down, and we ordered, talking easily about work. It was nice to talk to someone who didn't know me, or all my intricate details. Gra—no. I stopped myself. I wasn't thinking about him.

"So tell me about your partner. You talk about her a lot. Are you related?" Declan's head was cocked to one side, and he looked delicious.

I felt my neck warm at the thought.

"No," I said, forcing a laugh. "We went to law school together, and I asked her if she'd be my partner in our third year. She's fantastic," I added. "Even now that she's a newlywed."

Declan laughed. "Is she all, 'You should get married'? All my friends who do are immediately ready to hook up all their poor single friends."

"No, thankfully not. I think she knows better. Although it's hard," I added. "Our other friend, Xavier, just got married, and I'm the last one to be single. No one, including him, thought he'd ever get married again." I smiled, thinking about X. He and Olivia were perfect for each other.

Another Dhameer success story. Where was mine?

I wondered what the hell I was doing wrong, and when I'd find what my friend had.

"I'm sorry?" I came back to the conversation. I'd never find anything if I kept zoning out on dates.

"Two weddings in one year? The nagging is about to start."

"My mom is already there," I said. "I'm the only one who's single out of all the kids."

"How many?"

"I have two brothers."

"Does your family know?"

The conversation took a turn. Even though he asked it casually, it was a loaded question.

"That I'm gay? Well, yeah, they know now."

His eyebrows went up. "When did you tell them?"

I sighed. "About two months ago."

To my surprise, he laughed. "How did you keep it to yourself for so long? As soon as I got into college, my sisters confronted me."

"How many sisters?"

"Three. I didn't have a chance."

"Your family okay with it?" I found myself wondering how others had managed it.

He shrugged as he smiled although his gaze slid away. "Sure, why not? They just want me to be happy, although my mom told me she worried, because it made things harder for me. What about your family?"

"I don't think I gave them enough credit," I confessed. Part of me wondered if this was normal date conversation. "When I told them, everyone but one of my sisters-in-law was fine, and my brothers had a bet on it."

Declan laughed. "It's amazing how we struggle, and then we tell people, and they're not shocked."

I nodded. "I think it was a bit of a shock, because my family is pretty traditional."

"Well, couldn't they get a hint from your friends?"

I thought about that. "I don't really hang out with a lot of gay people," I said. "I used to hang out with—well, someone else, but they just thought he was one of my close friends, and we didn't—"

"They didn't know you were dating your ex?" There was pity in his face.

"No."

Declan looked down, and took a few bites of his food, then back at me, an earnest expression on his face.

"How old are you, Bryant?"

"Twenty-eight. Why?"

He sighed. "You're a grown man, but you've only just come out to your family. You don't hang out with a group of friends who get you. You're pretty contained. And you've just ended a long-term relationship. I like you. But I'm not sure we're in the same place."

I was stunned. I didn't even know what to say.

"What are you saying?"

Declan shrugged. "I don't know what I'm saying. There's a lot going on over there," he waved his hand in a circle at me. "I think it's hard to take on anything new with all that you're dealing with."

"So… are you saying that you'd rather not see me?" Holy shit. I didn't expect this.

"No, that's not what I'm saying. I'm saying that I look at things objectively and see where the potential challenges are. It's part of who I am," he grinned, and his smile was like a beacon. "I don't mind a challenge. I never have." He looked at me, right in the eyes.

It was intense. My neck got hot again, and I could feel myself crazily, intensely attracted to him.

"But you're a pretty big one. I don't think it's a deal breaker," he looked down at his food again. "I just believe in being honest with what I see."

"Yeah, you're that," I said.

His expression changed. "Oh, fuck. I didn't—" he looked away.

"What?" I felt like he was two steps ahead of me.

He looked back, a rueful expression on his face. "I didn't mean to lay my thought process on you. I'm really bad about it. I don't mind seeing where problems are. It makes things easier to navigate, to me. But not everyone is like that. I'm sorry."

What? I shook my head. This was a lot. "No, it's fine. I think—"

Declan held up a hand. "Since we're hitting all the heavy topics tonight, I'll just tell you that this little habit of mine has been a reason that all my exes have wanted to kill me at one time or another. They tell me it's defeatist."

"Well, it's a little intimidating," I said.

He laughed. "I'm sorry. How about we leave it at we both have shit, and we have to do what anyone else does, and work through the past shit to move forward?"

With those simple words, he eased all the discomfort I was feeling. "I like that. Tib tells me I'm baggage boy."

He laughed again. "She sounds fun."

I smiled, feeling normal for the first time since we'd started down this conversational minefield. "She is. She's my best friend."

"And who's the other guy?"

"X? Xavier. He's…" I hesitated.

"What? Now I'm overly curious."

"Well, you know who XTC is?"

"Yeah?"

He didn't make the connection.

"That's X. XTC."

A moment, and then his mouth opened slightly. "What? XTC? Really? Holy crap! How is that, being friends with someone that famous?"

I laughed. "He's kind of a pain in the ass. He and Tib grew up together. I inherited his friendship although I love the guy." I started laughing harder. "He's actually a lot of fun, in spite of the pain in the ass thing. You see where he ended up at Cobalt a while back?"

He nodded. "I read about that. I actually had a couple of friends who were there. They said—wait, were you there with him?"

I nodded. "We were taking Seth—that's Tibby's husband—out before the wedding, you know, as Tibby's best friends. That kind of thing. So we go out, and we're at a bar drinking whiskey, and we all get a little shitty, and then X says, You choose, Bry, and I went there." I laughed, thinking about it. "He had this huge bar bill, and numbers in all his pockets. He doesn't remember much, but his manager went ballistic."

"I can totally see the numbers. He's hot," Declan said.

"He is, but I don't even see it anymore," I said. "I've known him so long."

Declan started to laugh. "My friends that were there said he was wasted, but that he was so much fun. Then all the rumors started," he laughed some more.

"That's what pissed his manager off so much."

"I saw that statement he made. Was that why he did it?"

"Yeah, the guy was a total bigot, and X was not in the best mood, so he went out and fired him. Then he called me on the way home and said I had to help him find a new manager." I laughed. "I tried to say that was Tib's job, but he said the bar was my pick, and we weren't calling Tib on her honeymoon, so I got to it."

"That's what you do for friends," he said, laughing with me. "Even if it's a complete pain in the ass."

"Declan! Hey, man, what's going on?"

We both turned at the same time, and a stunningly handsome man was approaching the table. Declan got up, his hand out.

"Hey, Steve, how are you?"

"Good, good, man! Where you been? We haven't seen you in ages." Steve glanced at me.

Declan saw it. "Oh, sorry. Steve, this is my friend Bryant Higgs. Bryant, Steve Carter."

Steve stuck his hand out. "Bryant, good to meet you." We shook. Then he turned his attention back to Declan. "You coming out this week? You're like a hermit."

"I think so," Declan said. "It's been hell at work, and I haven't been able to get out in time to make it. We play pick up every week," he said to me. "And I'm a shit team member, because I haven't been there in what? Three weeks?"

Steve nodded. "We're all feeling like you dumped us," he pulled a sad face.

Declan laughed. "More like you got your ass handed to you and you're tired of losing. I'm the star player," he said to me as though he was confiding a secret.

"You wish," Steve laughed. "You think you can get away this week?"

"I'll try," Declan nodded.

"Hey, let me know, okay? That way we can manage our disappointment. You play?" Steve said to me.

"Play what?" I asked.

"Basketball? We have an easy-going league," Steve said. "You're welcome, if you'd like."

"He works more than I do," Declan said before I could answer.

"Well, if you guys can drag yourselves from your desks, maybe I'll see you." Steve turned, and waved at a couple of guys standing near the door. "All right, well, good seeing you, Deck. Bryant, good to meet you." He smiled and walked away.

Declan sat back down and looked at me. "I hope I

didn't overstep. I didn't want you to feel like you had to say yes. But you're welcome to come, if you'd like."

"I haven't played since college," I said.

"We're not really good, or anything. It's just fun, hanging out with the guys. I've missed it, but I really have been up to my ass in work. You should come though. It would be good for you to get out, meet people."

I felt the side of my mouth turn up. "I think you have a little cruise director in you, Declan."

He stared at me for a moment and then burst out laughing. "No one's ever called me that before, but I think it's an apt description. I'll have to tell my sisters." He chuckled.

Conversation moved away to less involved things, and I was grateful. This already felt like a lot to share.

But it was nice that I wasn't the only one with a baggage cart as Tib would say.

---

*A*fter we'd eaten until I thought I might burst— there was something about steamed mussels that made it hard for me to stop—Declan grabbed the bill before I could even make a move.

"Hey, let me," I began.

"Nope. This is on me. Next one's on you."

"All right, but no sneaking the bill on me," I warned.

"Well, at least this way I know we're having another date," he said, not meeting my eyes.

"Why wouldn't we?"

Declan looked up from the bill as he put his card down. "You don't think we got a little involved in our conversation? I don't regret it, but I will if you decide you don't want to see me again."

"I thought I was the one who was all messed up," I said.

"Everyone's messed up, Bryant. It's just a matter of what's your poison."

I felt that warm feeling again, the one I'd felt before. Like I wasn't alone, I wasn't a freak would die alone, with no one discovering me until the smell bothered the neighbors.

Hey, it's a legit fear.

"I think there will be another date," I said, warmed by how nice this felt.

"Good. I'm glad to know I didn't fuck it all up. But let's just stay low-key and honest, okay?"

"Okay," I said.

We got up and headed out.

"You want to walk for a bit?" Declan asked

"Yeah, I ate too much. It's the mussels," I added.

"I know. It's hard to stop."

Jesus God. I felt about one hundred, having this conversation, but we headed down toward the canal. It was a good place.

Neither of us spoke very much, and as we headed onto the path, the street lights spaced out. It was darker, and I was surprised how comfortable I felt with him. I didn't think that I'd find that again—well, at least not so soon after—well. Not just yet.

Censuring your thoughts was a pain in the ass.

As we walked along, the silence stretched out. Then Declan stopped and grabbed my hand.

"I know it might not be the best move, but I've wanted to do this all night," he said, and his voice was husky. "Slap me if I'm being an asshole," and he pulled me close.

His other hand went up to my face and caressed my

cheek. "You are the most handsome man I've met in ages," he whispered.

He hesitated, his lips close to mine. I could practically feel the sparks between us, but he didn't get any closer.

I reached up and put my hands on his face, bringing him closer. "You're anything but an asshole," I said as I kissed him.

The electricity that I felt being near him that I'd felt when he took my hand on our first date was nothing—nothing—compared to this. I felt it race through me, ending at my toes. I immediately got hard, and I could feel the blood rushing in my brain.

His arms went around me, tightening his hold on me. He had a slight stubble across his jaw, a little five o'clock shadow, and the feel of it against my face made my heart race even faster.

His tongue licked at my lips, and it was like throwing gasoline on a fire. I wanted to tear his clothes off and spend the entire night with him, exploring every inch of him.

I couldn't remember the last time I'd felt overwhelmed by desire. It wasn't just desire though—it was that this amazing, handsome, sexy man was kissing me, and apparently having the same thoughts I was. The idea that I made him as hot as he made me just upped my desire to drag him to the nearest room.

He ran one of his hands up my back, and neck and then into my hair and I felt my knees get weak. He smelled so good, and his lips were firm, and he touched me like I was the only thing in the world.

We stumbled a bit, back into a small fence, and then broke apart, both breathing heavily.

"Wow," Declan said.

"Yeah," I said.

He laughed softly. "So much for taking things all slow,"

"It was slow enough," I said. "It can count."

"So says the lawyer," he took my hand as he said it, and I could see the flash of his smile even in the darkness. "Listen, why don't we head back?"

I smiled, even though everything below the waistline was screaming for another call. "Okay."

We held hands as we walked back toward the restaurant.

"This is me," I said, pointing at my car.

"Well, thank you for a great evening," Declan said.

He squeezed my hand, and I wrapped my free hand around his waist, unable to resist him. Our lips met, and the same feeling of flying and adrenaline raced through me. It hadn't gone away, but a little physical distance allowed my heart rate to go back to normal for a moment.

No more. I felt myself falling into him, and I didn't want to stop. But I needed to. I stepped back, breathless. "Thank you for a great evening," I said.

"I'll call you?" I could hear the slight question.

"Yes."

He kissed me again, once on the lips, light and gentle. Then with another squeeze of my hand, he let it go and walked away. I watched him, admiring him as he did.

Then I leaned against the car and tried to catch my breath.

Holy shit. I hadn't expected that.

As I drove home, I thought about it. I hadn't expected to feel such naked lust for anyone other than Graham, and certainly not anytime soon. But Declan was really fantastic, and I enjoyed him. You know, even putting my raging hard-on aside.

It made me wonder at the depth of my feelings for Graham. Not that I was holding out hope for him—okay, maybe a little. Everyone wants their ex to come back, weeping tears of regret and groveling for forgiveness.

Or maybe that was just me. I'd have to ask Tib if I was just shittier than most people.

Declan's comments made me think about the fact that I was really pretty alone. I'd stayed aloof from a lot of the family friends because while we were living in a fairly enlightened society, one just didn't "do" gay—even if it wasn't a big deal anymore everywhere else. I didn't want to have someone stumble on my secret.

I had Tib, and X, but Declan was right. I didn't go out with a lot of people like me—preferring to keep my private life private. Or so I told myself.

Graham and I used to go out together, but he had friends he went out with that were his friends before we met. I'd always found them more superficial than I liked, so after hanging out with them initially, I'd stopped.

When I'd taken Seth and X to Cobalt, it was because it was a place that Graham and I loved to go to dance. I liked being in a large, anonymous crowd.

I'd spent a lot of my life not only being in the closet, but being comfortable doing it. My family showed me that I didn't have to stay there, but not everyone was accepting.

As Melissa and my dad's client showed.

But the family didn't care. Tib and X didn't care. If I kept dating Declan—were we dating? If we kept going out, I got the impression that he wasn't going to be content with me being half in, half out of the closet.

And from his point of view, I got it.

That didn't change the fact that I'd been shoved into something I'd never thought about, and it was still a world that I wasn't comfortable with.

Well, I needed to make some changes. Graham might have been a weasel in the end, but his argument about not hiding who he was, who we were together—it had merit.

Even though just fuck him for being a cheating weasel.

Sometimes being a lawyer sucked. You could see both sides without too much trouble, and it was hard to get all indignant.

But I could get indignant about the cheating. He didn't have the courtesy to just end it. He kept me strung out and dancing to make him happy, even as he knew he'd never give me what I wanted.

When had he started to hate me? Because that's how you treated people you hated, not loved. I thought that Pricilla, my sister-in-law, might be right when she said I'd dodged a bullet. Just because same-sex marriage was new didn't mean that divorce was any less expensive.

Enough of Graham. He needed to be he-who-is-a-cheating-weasel-ass-and-not-mentioned. It was time to look forward, to look at Declan.

In spite of he-who-is-a-weasel's comments, Declan found me attractive, and appealing, and hopefully as sexy as I found him.

He knew I was a part-time mess, and he didn't seem to mind. He-who-is-a-weasel made everything sound like my fault. While I had them, certainly, I didn't own all the faults between us.

I pulled into my parking space at the townhouse, and got out, still thinking.

I'd need to make some changes. I couldn't go back in the closet. I didn't have to be wearing a pride flag and thigh high patent leather boots, but I could find a balance where I kept my private life to myself, but still allowed myself to be seen as what I was.

A man who'd just had the best date of my life.

So how to move on from here?

16

$\mathcal{I}$t turned out that the way to move on was to force yourself out of the house and to interact with other people. Again, it was one of those things that I'd never seen as a problem, but I was more of a shut-in than I'd thought.

Declan called me Saturday night after our date, and we went to the movies. I don't even remember what we saw, as I was focused on holding his hand, and sitting close to him in the dark theater.

We ended up making out again that night, although it was Declan that pulled away this time, and I left him at his car.

I joined him and his friends for basketball later the next week.

Tibby caught me as I was changing.

"What—or rather, where are you going?"

"I'm getting together with some guys for basketball."

Her mouth fell open. "I didn't know that you were into that."

"I didn't either, but Declan invited me."

She crossed her arms, smiled at me like a cat who ate the canary, and said, "Well, don't try to be the star. You'll hurt like hell the next day. Have fun," and she left.

I found that once again, I was nervous when I got to the gym where he said they played. I walked in, and I saw Steve from the restaurant.

"Bryant!" He waved me over. "Hey, man, glad you could make it. You know if Declan's coming?"

"He said he was," I said, feeling shy. I wasn't sure we were a couple, or even anything other than make out partners. I certainly didn't want to speak for him.

"Great. This is Mark, Tomas, and Heath," he indicated the three men he was talking to.

I shook hands all around, but was saved from awkward small talk when Declan came up behind me and patted me on the shoulder. "Bryant, I'm glad you were able to get away. He works for a taskmaster," he said to the other guys.

They laughed. A few more minutes, and the game got going.

I checked out the guys we were playing against. They all seemed to be friends, and I'd bet every one of them was gay.

This was both nice, and weird. I didn't hang out with a lot of gay guys. More of that whole 'let's stay in the closet forever' thing.

I was finding being with Declan both fun and challenging. Thankfully, the challenges hadn't been that difficult.

Well, other than being completely trashy and wanting to go to bed with him too soon, and fighting that impulse.

Dating had been a nightmare when I was younger, not only because I was dating the sex I wasn't truly attracted to. It was still kind of a nightmare, because I wanted to be all trashy, but I didn't really know what the proper etiquette was. Which made me laugh. Of course I'd be looking at the etiquette of it all. I needed to loosen up. I wanted to. It was a matter of how much.

The games that night were so much fun I joined them for the next two weeks. At the end of the third night, I sat on the bench, wiping my face with a towel, and getting a drink. These nights were fun. Everyone went out for a beer afterward, and I found that I enjoyed that just as much.

They treated Declan and I as a couple although it was really low-key. Since he and I hadn't progressed much beyond hot make out sessions, I was okay with that. Although I wasn't sure for how much longer—feeling his body pressed up against mine was sending my self-control right on out the window.

Happy thoughts of how to move things along were foremost in my mind as I looked out across the gym.

Then I nearly choked on my water.

Coming into the gym under the arm of an enormous guy was Graham.

"You all right?" Declan asked, noticing me half-choking.

"I'm good," I said as soon as I got myself together. "We heading out?" I really, really didn't want to—what? See Graham up close? Have him see me? I wasn't sure, but I didn't want to face it, or him.

"Yeah, let's go," he took my hand as he stood up, pulling me with him. "You guys ready?" He asked the others.

To a chorus of yes's, we headed out. *Please, please*, I begged whatever deity might be listening, *don't let Graham see me*. I could feel my palm sweating, and I hoped that Declan didn't notice.

No such fucking luck.

Graham and his giant accessory stopped, and he

looked me up and down, a sardonic grin on his face. "Bryant, isn't this a surprise?"

"Yeah, it is. But we're done, so see you later," I said, struggling not to glare at him. Seeing him now, up close, after all I'd learned about what he'd been up to, and what he'd piled onto me made me want to knock the shit-eating grin right off his face.

Preferably into the next state.

"Who's your friend?" Graham asked.

God, had he always sounded so nasal and catty?

"This is my friend Declan. Declan, this is a former friend of mine, Graham."

Graham's eyes widened. Oh, I thought snidely. I guess I was supposed to be pining still? Not ever again.

Graham stuck out his hand, and Declan took it. I liked that Declan definitely won in a comparison side-by-side.

"Good to meet you," Declan said, no trace of anything in his voice. "We're on the way out, so have a good evening."

I noticed no one introduced the giant. Probably the taxi, I thought, still being snide.

Then Declan moved, and I walked with him. I felt him squeeze my hand, and some anger over the bullshit that I'd just stepped in faded. I'd done it. I'd come across Graham, and didn't fall apart, didn't make an ass of myself, and didn't come off as needy and pathetic.

Neither of us spoke as we walked out of the gym. We got to my car, and I tossed my gear in.

"You okay?" Declan asked.

"Yeah," I said.

"That the ex?"

"Yeah," I said. "Sorry if that was awkward at all."

Declan didn't speak, and then I felt him next to me,

and his hand was at the base of my skull cupping it, pulling me to him. He kissed me fiercely, holding nothing back.

I forgot that we were in a public area, and I kissed him in the same way, letting all the things I felt for him, and the frustration that we hadn't gotten any further than kissing fall into the kiss.

"You wanna skip beers tonight?"

"I have a nice bar at my place," I said.

"Perfect. I'll follow you," he said.

He stalked away, and I watched him. There was something different about him, something that was all business, take no shit take no prisoners.

I had a feeling we were going to move beyond the make out stage tonight. Which was fine with me.

But I wondered what prompted it. He'd been so reserved. I thought about it as I drove home. I tried not to speed in my haste to get there.

Declan found parking on the street and joined me as I was unlocking the door. He came up behind me, one arm around my waist grabbing me between the legs, and the other across my shoulders. He kissed the back of my neck and I felt myself go up in flames.

He was so damn sexy.

We fell into my front door, all hands and fumbling as we tore at one another's clothing. First my shirt, and then his, and I felt his hot skin next to mine. He was still warm from the gym, and I could feel the sheen of sweat across his chest.

It was delicious, and it thrilled me.

"I've wanted to see you naked for weeks," he murmured into my mouth.

"That makes two of us," I said, backing him up as we kissed.

"Where are we going?" He asked, chuckling as we

bumped into the couch.

"The bedroom."

"Where?"

I pointed up the narrow stairs at the back of the room. He kicked off his shoes, and together, we walked up the stairs. I led him to my room, and when we stepped in the doorway, he wrapped his arms around me, kissing me until I thought I was going fall over.

I had never, ever felt this way with anyone else.

"You're wearing too many clothes," I said. I pulled at the string of his shorts.

Declan stepped back, and without taking his eyes from mine, he hooked his thumbs in his waistband and pushed the shorts and his boxers down.

Oh my holy God. His cock sprang out, showing that he was just as excited about this as I was.

"Now who's wearing too many clothes?" He grinned at me.

I was out of my clothes faster than I thought possible. As my shorts hit the floor, I was reaching for Declan, wanting to feel his skin next to mine. I ran my hands through his hair, and then down his back, stopping to grab the ass I'd been watching for what seemed like ages.

It felt as good as it looked. The thought made me grin even as I kissed him.

It was like when you were in high school, and you were so desperate to be with the person you were with that you wanted to crawl inside their skin.

I let my hands come around the front of him, taking his cock in both hands.

He let out a noise that was a cross between a sigh and a hiss.

"That feels so good," he whispered.

"I've wanted to touch you for weeks," I said.

"Thank God. I thought it might just be me."

"No. It wasn't just you," I said, kissing him again. I walked backwards a few steps until I reached my bed, falling onto it and bringing him with me. His body felt so good against mine.

"Tell me you have a condom," Declan groaned.

"Oh, hell yes," I said.

"More than one?" His eyes opened, and he looked at me. The corner of his mouth lifted.

"Yeah, why?"

"Because we're going to need them."

"All of them?" I asked. I was thrilled and astounded to hear the teasing note in my voice along with the hunger for him.

"We can try." He laughed. "We're not going to sleep yet. Not for quite a while, in fact."

Those were the best words I'd heard in a long time. True to his promise, we didn't get to sleep until much, much later.

I woke up just as dawn was breaking through the window and started slightly. There was someone in my bed. It took me a moment to remember who it was, and as I did, I could feel a grin spread across my face.

Declan stirred, and lazily moved an arm up toward me, reaching for me to bring me closer. I let myself relax into his arm. He felt good. He felt *right*.

I closed my eyes and savored the feeling.

Then I went back to sleep.

---

*T*he phone rang. It kept ringing. Squinting at the sunlight, I got up and reached for my shorts.

"Yeah?"

"You alive?" Tibby asked.

"Yes. I mean, of course. What time is it?"

"You're not late, if that's what you're wondering. But you didn't call me last night, and I think you hit your five-date limit. So you have to tell me everything, and you guys are having dinner with me and Seth this weekend."

"What if I don't want to, bossy britches?"

"Well, we don't always get what we want, do we? Get up and get a shower. Otherwise you're going to be late, slacker." She hung up.

"What time is it?"

I looked over at Declan, who was stretching with his eyes closed.

"According to my partner, we're not late, but we will be if we keep lying around like lazy asses," I said.

"Shit. I didn't mean to fall asleep," he said, sitting up.

"I'm glad you did," I said. Was he regretting this?

He turned his mega-watt smile to me. "I am too. But now I need to hustle, get to work."

"You can shower here. Borrow whatever you need," I said, surprising myself. I didn't like to share clothes, but it came out without me even thinking about it.

"I don't want to be weird, but in the interest of time, I think I will. Thanks, Bryant," he said, swinging his legs out of bed. He headed for the bathroom.

God, I could watch him walk forever. He was graceful and sleek. Today, he moved like a panther. How had I not noticed this before?

Maybe it was the good sex? I laughed quietly to myself.

I know it was the good sex for me although I didn't know if I would look that hot walking.

I heard the shower start, and I pulled on the shorts, heading down to get the coffee started. At least this wasn't weird or anything.

By the time I had a pot of coffee made, and pulled out some stuff for breakfast, Declan had finished his shower, and he came down the stairs wrapped in a towel.

I nearly said fuck work and dragged him back upstairs. The water glistening on his chest and shoulders, his dark hair wet and messy—he took my breath away.

"Thank God. You made a whole pot," he said.

"Yeah, help yourself." I found it hard to talk. He was so beautiful.

"I wasn't sure what you wanted to share, and I didn't want to be that guy going through all your shit," he said.

"Um, okay, let me grab you some stuff. I'll go get it," I said, hurrying upstairs before I lost all control.

What the hell was happening to me? I was never like this. I kept myself under control. I didn't make scenes. Everything was discreet, and tasteful.

Declan blew all those norms right out of the water. I didn't even care.

I pulled out some clothes and then sent myself to the shower. I didn't trust myself otherwise. Declan came in while I was in the shower.

The door to the shower was glass, and I could see him watching me on the other side.

"Hey," he said.

I stopped giving him the side eye and looked over. "Yeah?"

"You are sex on a stick. You wanna play hooky today?"

Oh my God. I didn't answer right away, stunned and thrilled that he was thinking the same things I was. I guess he thought I was hesitating, because he dropped his towel, and came to the door, pressing himself up against it.

"This could be all yours," he said. Then he slowly turned around, plastering himself against the shower door. He looked over his shoulder and winked and blew me a kiss. "Interested?"

In answer, I opened the shower door and yanked him in with me. I was rock hard, to the point that I was aching. My hands were on his cock as fast as his were on mine. But I had a plan. I dropped to my knees and took him in my mouth.

"Oh, God," he moaned, throwing his head back. "Jesus, Bryant."

I didn't answer. I wanted him to lose control, to bring him to the same place that I was. I sucked harder, not wanting to take my time, or give him time to do anything but hang on.

We were in the shower until the water went cold. It was only through serious focus and staying away from each other that we made it out of my place on time to get to work.

"Call me tonight," he said. "I mean it. I want to see you tonight."

"I will."

"You're not getting away from me, Higgs," he said teasingly.

Right there on my street, in front of my house, I kissed him. "I don't want to."

"Good thing. I'd hate to go all stalker."

"Go to work before you make me late. I don't want to hear it from Tib."

"Ah, yes. The hard ass."

"Yeah, laugh it up," I said. "You get to meet her this weekend."

His eyes widened. "What?"

I waved a hand at him. "Not so funny now, huh? It's okay—we'll talk tonight, okay?"

"Way to scare the shit out of me," he muttered.

"It will be fine," now I was laughing.

I was still smiling when I rolled into work. Of course, Tibby was the first person I saw.

17

"Oh, holy hell," she muttered, her coffee cup halfway to her lips. She was at the desk of one of our paralegals, Darcy. "Darce, can this wait a bit?" Tibby didn't take her eyes off me.

"Sure," Darcy said. "Hey, Bryant. You look good today," she added.

"He sure does," Tibby said. "I think we need to have a little conference before we get going today," she said to me.

"I don't know why," I breezed by her. "I'm getting some coffee, and then I must get to work," I dodged Tibby making a grab for me, which was saying something considering she had coffee in one hand.

I heard Darcy laugh as I escaped to the break room. Tibby was hot on my heels. I didn't turn around as I fixed my coffee. When I finally did, she was standing in front of the door.

"You're going to tell. All of it."

"All of what?" I smiled innocently.

"All of everything. Because everything is written all over you. What number date was last night?"

I shrugged. "I don't know." But I did. It was eleven. I'd seen him at the basketball games, and we'd seen each other during those three weeks since we'd gone to Maxime. I just hadn't told her.

For this very reason.

"It's more than five. So now you get to spill."

"What if I don't want to?"

"It doesn't work that way, Bryant. You dated, now tell." She turned and marched to her office.

I followed her. There was no way I wouldn't tell, but I was having fun teasing her. I did, however, make sure to close the door behind me as we entered her office.

Tibby threw herself in her chair—how the hell did she manage that without spilling her coffee, I wondered.

"Tell."

I recognized my negotiating partner. The one who made opposing attorneys groan because she took no shit, and no prisoners.

I smiled, because despite that, I knew she'd be thrilled for me.

"I had a fantastic date last night."

"Did you sleep with him?"

I nodded. "Several times, in fact."

"And?" Her expression was unreadable.

"It was incredible. Fucking incredible, Tib. I haven't felt like that with someone in... I can't even remember when." I stopped, taking a drink of my coffee. I knew what I wanted to say, but I was nervous to say it. Tibby knew me, and she would know what I was saying. "I was so uptight with Graham, and there was always so much other shit with us—"

"I didn't know it was that bad."

I nodded. "I didn't either, but being with Declan is like seeing relationships in a completely different light." I didn't add that I was doing a shit ton of soul searching to boot. No need to give her all the juicy aspects right this second.

We did need to get to work at some point.

"And it blows my mind," I continued. "So last night… oh God."

"What?"

"We were at the basketball court in the gym, and right as we finished and were heading out, Graham came in with some huge beefcake."

"Jesus, that guy is like herpes," Tibby muttered. "He doesn't ever leave, does he? It's not like we live in a small town or something."

"Yeah, he does keep turning up."

"Okay, so what happened?"

"I introduced him to Declan—and he didn't introduce me to the beefcake, and we left."

"And?"

"And then we went back to my place and had the hottest sex I have ever had in my life. I don't even know why it happened like that. It was like an explosion or something. He was on a mission when we got to my place." I thought about it. Something had been driving him, and while I wasn't complaining, I wondered what it was.

"You guys didn't talk?"

"Pshaw," I said, taking a gruff tone. "That's wimmenz stuff."

"Whatever," she rolled her eyes. "So you have no idea what moved things from make out to hot sex?"

"It was about time? It's been over a month."

Tibby shook her head. "No, there was something else."

"I hate it when you're right," I muttered.

"I wish you'd remember I'm usually right," she grumbled. "What do you think it is?"

"I have no idea, but I suppose we'll talk about it. Now that you brought it up and put that maggot in my head."

"It was already there, so hold your fire," she said.

"Yeah, it was. And I'm not complaining. I was ready to move to something more than crazy making out. It made me feel like a teenager again."

Tibby grinned. "That's not always a bad thing, Bry."

"Maybe not for you. I was thrilled to get out of my teenage years."

"I swear, you're like twenty-eight going on fifty sometimes."

"One of us has to be the adult," I shot back. This wasn't anything new.

"Okay, go to work," she said abruptly.

"That's it?" I asked.

"What do you mean?"

"Don't you want more of the post-mortem?"

Tibby laughed. "I would love it, but I know who I'm dealing with. And it's no good trying to get you to talk feelings. I'd bet you're just starting to figure them out for yourself. I think this guy could be good for you. I'm seeing a different side of you. A more relaxed side. But I'll reserve judgement until this weekend."

"I didn't say we were coming."

"Like you're going to turn me down," Tibby scoffed. "Please."

"How about you let me ask him, and then I'll let you know?"

"Well, I suppose." She sighed dramatically.

"Thank you, boss."

"Think nothing of it."

I got up. At the door I stopped and looked back at her. "I love you, you know."

"I know. Love you, too, stuffed shirt."

Things were back to normal. She wouldn't interrogate me again until after I brought Declan by for inspection.

Although part of me wondered why I cared so much what Tibby thought, I knew that I was looking forward to this. I wanted her to see us together, to tell me what she saw.

Because I knew I'd never felt this way before. I hoped it showed to the point that other people saw it.

And as Tibby said, we still had to have the sex talk. And oh hell. The ex talk. And who knew what else?

Despite all that, I wasn't worried.

It was a novel, and enjoyable feeling. Which kept me smiling all day.

My cell rang later that day, and when I saw that it was him on the caller ID, my smile got larger. I didn't know how it was possible.

"Hey," I answered it, my voice warm.

"Hey, yourself. What time are you free?"

"I can be out of here by five, five-thirty at the latest."

"Good. Can I cook you dinner tonight?"

"I'd love it," I said.

"Great. I'm going to text my address. Come over when you're done."

"Okay."

"I can't wait to see you," he added.

"I can't wait to see you," I said.

"Great. All right, I'll see you tonight."

I heard the promise in his voice, and I could feel the heat from last night shoot through me like he was standing next to me.

The end of the day couldn't come fast enough. When it finally hit five, I said, "Fuck it." I closed down my laptop and put all my files away. I stuck my head in Tibby's door on the way out.

"I'm leaving."

"Okay. Don't be a hussy."

"Whatevs," I rolled my eyes and left, hearing her laughter behind me.

Declan didn't live far from the office, or me. That was nice. I drove over, sizing up the parking. I'm not kidding— you have to take parking into account everywhere you go here. I found a spot on his block, and I headed for his place.

It was hard not to run. When was the last time I'd been this excited?

I thought about that, and the answer wasn't something I wanted to think about at the moment, so I pushed it aside. I ran lightly up the stairs to his place and pushed the doorbell, hearing the pounding of my own heart.

A moment and then Declan opened the door with that smile on his face that could light up the world.

"Right on time," he said. He reached for me and gave me a small kiss as he drew me in the door. "Come in."

I followed him in, looking around as I did so. I liked a simple, clean look. It had been the despair of Tibby when we lived together. But I liked as little clutter as possible. It made it easier for me to relax.

Declan's home was fairly simple, but he liked warmer colors than I did. The kitchen was in the back of the house, and as I came in, I saw that the kitchen was one that a foodie would have. That could be a good thing. Like the rest of the house I'd seen so far, it was simple and clean.

"Wine?" He waved a bottle at me.

"Yes, please," I said. I found that I was nervous, and I didn't know exactly why. I mean, I knew why, but as to which aspect… it could be several. "Is this yours?"

He looked around with a smile. "No, it's rented. I

wasn't sure how long I'd be here, so the company helped me find a place. I like it though. It's simple."

He handed me a glass of something red, and I took a bigger drink than I planned because I still had a case of the nerves, which made me choke.

"You all right?" Declan was all concern.

I held up a hand, covering my mouth as I coughed. I was all sorts of smooth, I thought.

"Sorry," I said when I caught my breath. "Went down the wrong way."

"Oh, well, good. I'd hate to think I had shitty wine," he said with a smile. "But that suggests I'm glad you nearly choked to death in my kitchen."

We both laughed.

"Here. Sit." Declan pointed to the small island. He went to the sink and brought me back a glass of water before he moved back toward the stove.

"So you want to talk now, get it out of the way?" He asked. His back was to me, and his tone was casual.

Oh, he was good. "Okay."

"I don't think we were rushing things last night," he said to the pot he leaned over.

"I don't think so either."

"But I got the feeling it surprised you," he said. At that he turned and looked at me, eyebrows raised.

"It did," I said. "I'm not complaining, but I wasn't expecting sex last night."

"Make my ego feel better and tell me that you were at least thinking about it," he said, and I could hear the laughter in his words.

"Oh, God, yes."

"Thank God. I didn't want to be the only sex mad one."

"Not even close," I said fervently.

"It was incredible," he turned around again. There wasn't a hint of humor anywhere on him.

"Yes, it was," I smiled.

"But unexpected. For me, anyway. I wanted to talk to you about it."

"What is there to say?"

"Was that your ex we met at the gym?"

I was so glad his back was to me. "Yes."

"God, he was really shitty," Declan glanced over his shoulder again. "I'm sorry. And I could see that he wanted to be cruel. You handled it well, by the way."

I sighed. "Thank you. It was pretty shitty. I was surprised, because he wasn't like that with me, but there are things…" I stopped. How far did I want to go with this? Be honest, Declan had told me. I'd spent my whole life hiding. Being less than honest.

"Well, he wasn't the person I thought he was. Honestly, he pissed me off. Rather than make a scene which I think he would have liked, I decided to get the hell out of there."

"Who ended it?"

"He did."

"Did you ask him to try again?"

How did he know this? Or was I just that transparent? "I did."

"Yeah, I thought so. Some guys just can't resist being an asshole about the whole thing. Sorry to disappoint you, but we won't run into any of my exes here," he grinned at me.

"I think I can live with the disappointment," I said dryly.

"I'm making a mess of this," Declan said, turning around and putting his hands on the island. "I wasn't smooth at all, and I kept worrying that you'd think I was a pushy bastard, or something like that. But I saw your face,

I knew that guy was out to hurt you, and I wanted you to know that whatever he was trying to tell you, it's not true."

I opened my mouth, but I didn't say anything. I didn't know what to say. No one had ever said anything so kind, so loving, to me.

"I don't even know what he was trying to say, but it was bitchy and cruel, and I couldn't stand it." Declan looked worried.

I set down the glass I'd been holding and took his hand. "I'm glad you did it. I was starting to go crazy with figuring out how to make the next move. You know, after I told you my sad tale, and…"

Declan held up a hand. "I asked you for honesty. That means always, not just when it's convenient. Exes are never convenient," he added.

"Yeah, you can say that again," I said.

"Okay, so we're all good?"

"Yes, but if you don't feed me soon, we won't be."

"Oh, well your wish is my command," Declan smiled, and his voice was sultry.

My blood raced through me, and I fell into his eyes, lost in the blue like you'd see in the ocean.

"Then my command is to feed me," I answered, my voice a little ragged with all the things I wanted to do to him. With him.

He smiled.

We did manage to eat before having sex on the kitchen floor. And then in the bedroom, and the bathroom.

I fell asleep in his bed, Declan turned toward me. His breathing was soft, and I could tell he was asleep or nearly so. His arm was thrown over my waist. The smell of him was everywhere.

It felt right.

It felt like home.

he next couple of weeks were the best of my life. I didn't think about the wish I'd made, or what it meant, because I was too busy living. When I did think about it, my thoughts were wasn't this the point? To make changes, and live? I pushed thoughts of the wish aside.

Thankfully, Dhameer didn't put in an appearance. It would have forced something I wasn't ready for.

Everything with Declan was like learning it all over again. Not just the relationship aspects, but going out to a new restaurant, or taking a run along the canal together. He wasn't from the area, so we went up to Great Falls and took the canal boat tour. It was pulled by mules. We held hands on that trip, and for the first time, I didn't feel like everyone was looking at me, saying, there are the gay guys, and judging.

I didn't notice anyone look at me at all. Because I was too busy being me and being with my boyfriend.

It was a revelation.

Our dinner with Tibby and Seth had been fantastic,

and things had only gotten better from that point on. It felt like I was living in a fairy tale. I'd never been so happy.

I'd had dinner with my family in that time, and they all noticed the difference in me. I wasn't ready to tell them about Declan, what with Melissa still being an ass. I just said that I was moving on from my earlier disappointment, and I was glad that I didn't look as bad as I had been.

My mother squeezed my hand as I left the house and told me she loved me with a rather pointed look. There'd be time to tell her. I kissed her and told her I loved her too.

Truth was, I wasn't ready to share him. I wanted to enjoy life with just the two of us, getting to know him better, learning his likes (eggs benedict at any time of the day) and dislikes (he was allergic to dandelions. We laughed at how he'd discovered that—teasing his sisters and getting them shoved up his nose). I didn't want to have the world intrude just yet.

But as the priest says, Man proposes but God disposes. The world wouldn't be denied.

We were out on the patio at my house on a Saturday morning. Both of us were on our laptops. I was reading something from work, and I didn't know what he was doing. He made a noise, and I looked over. His brows were furrowed, a sure sign of distress. I'd been with him long enough to know that look.

Not that it had ever been directed at me.

"What?" I asked.

"It's from my mom."

"What's up?"

"My dad is in the hospital."

"Why didn't she call?"

"She said there are no cell phones allowed, and she doesn't want to cry on the phone with me. I have to go back, Bry," he said, looking up at me.

"Of course you do," I said. I reached over and touched his arm. It felt weird to be so sad when the sun shone and I was so happy, but I hurt for him. "What can I do?"

"Nothing, right now. I just need to get home. I'm going to book a flight tonight if I can."

"Okay," I said. I wondered if I should ask him if he wanted me to come with him and then stopped myself. He didn't need to be dealing with a new relationship when his dad was sick.

"Listen, if you need me, I'll be there the same day," I said. I wanted him to know he could count on me that I was there for him to lean on.

He shot me a grateful look. "I appreciate that. But as much as I'd love it, I'm going to pass right now. My mom will get all weird, and feel like she's supposed to be a hostess, and it will make me crazy." He laughed, but it wasn't a particularly happy sound. "You don't need to see all my family shit right now."

"Hey, you're talking to the baggage collector, remember?"

He smiled, but it was strained. He got up and took the laptop inside with him.

A cold thread of fear wound its way through me, but I dismissed it. I hoped that his dad would be okay.

I kissed him as I dropped him off at the airport that night. He'd protested, but I said no one wanted to take the Metro if they didn't have to. It was a long ride. He held my hand all the way there.

"Take care of yourself," he said. "You're bad about being too hard on yourself."

"You do the same," I said. I was worried. He wasn't the same guy I'd been getting to know these past couple of months.

"I'll call you," he kissed me once more.

"Okay. No rush. Let me know you got there all right and take care of your mom."

"I—" he stopped. "I'm going to miss you," he said.

I kissed him and held his face in my hands. "I'm here, whenever you need me. Take your time. I'll miss you, too."

He kissed me, and it was a hard, almost desperate kiss. Then he bolted from the car, stopping to look over his shoulder at me. I blew him a kiss, not caring if anyone saw. He smiled, but it was a painful smile.

Then he was gone.

Why did it feel like we'd just said goodbye? Not the kind of gone-on-a-trip type either, but more.

I shook my head. I was being ridiculous. I put the car in gear and headed home.

As I drove, I thought about how I wanted to ask him to move in when he got back. Or would it be too soon?

Declan texted me when he got in. He seemed stressed, so I didn't do anything other than text him back, letting him know once again that I was there if he needed me.

I felt lost on Sunday. I was used to being with him regularly, and time alone felt weird. Instead of moping, I cleaned the house, and went for a run as the sun was setting. When I got back, I saw that he'd called.

When I listened to the message, it was clear that things weren't going well.

"Hey, Bry, listen, this is not great, things aren't great right now. I'm outside the hospital, and my dad's heart is, they're not sure how long he's going to be in here—" his voice broke. "I'll call you again when I can. I'll be at the hospital most of the day, so if you don't hear from me, don't worry." He paused. "I miss you. I miss everything we have been building." Then he hung up.

How did he do that? He always seemed to be on the same wavelength as me. I felt a wave of tenderness, and more, wash over me at the thought of him. I wished that I could be there with him, but a new boyfriend is nothing to bring home to a sick bed and family drama.

I sent him a quick text to let him know that I'd gotten his message, and to call me when he could.

Then the work week started again. For once, since I'd met Declan, I was glad that we were neck deep in clients. It allowed me to not think about him although I missed him. I missed his smell, his touch, his laughter. Everything.

We texted all week, but on Thursday, he finally called.

"Hey! I'm so glad to catch up with you!" I said.

"Hey, how are you doing, Bry?" He sounded worn and tired.

"Better than you, from what it sounds like. How's your dad?"

"It's not good. I don't think he's coming out of here, although Mom and the family—well, they don't want to hear it. But that's where I think this is heading. It's heart failure, and… well, it's heart failure." I could hear his voice tremble a little.

"I'm so sorry. Do you want me to come out—?"

"No!" His answer was swift, almost harsh. Then his voice softened. "No, I don't think I could handle you seeing my family. They're very Midwestern, very traditional."

What did that mean? "Do they not accept you?"

"No, they accept me, but… it's complicated."

"You don't have to explain that to me, Declan. It's me, remember? King of complicated."

"Yeah, I knew you'd understand."

"I miss you," I said.

"I miss you, too," he whispered. "Listen," his voice rose, "I need to get going. I'll speak with you again."

And he hung up.

That was a bit off. Something wasn't right. Then I mentally kicked myself. Of course it wasn't right. His father was dying. No one else would accept it, which meant Declan had to deal with the coming loss of his father, as well as the burden of the family. I'd seen this when my grandmother had passed away. No one wanted to admit it, but she was dying. Didn't slow the death process down a bit to have people pretending it wasn't happening.

I mentally put my paranoia and foolishness away. I was reading things into things that weren't there. It came with the territory. I'd been burned, and I still had the scars to prove it. These kinds of things didn't heal as quickly as one might like.

Poor Declan. Given the apparent denial of his family, no wonder he insisted on honesty. Once more, I thanked whatever deity might be above watching, because I needed the honesty. After learning what I'd learned about Graham, I needed to know that my partner wasn't feeding me a line of bullshit.

The longer I was with Declan, the more I saw that things had been so skewed with Graham and me. While it hurt—boy, did it hurt—his turning me down was the best thing he'd ever done for me. Not only had it brought me Declan, but it had forced me to look within myself, to be honest with myself for probably the first time in my life.

When we'd first started dating, Declan's willingness to be openly affectionate put me off. Rather, it made me nervous. Which made me look at why I was so reluctant to even hold his hand in public.

It wasn't anything horrible. I certainly wasn't ashamed to be seen with him. It came to me, on one of my runs, that I was ashamed of me. Not anyone else. But me. Myself.

I'd grown up in a family where people weren't gay. Oh, there were probably some closeted gay folk floating around the family tree somewhere, but not out in the open. No one knew if there were. I knew I was gay early on. Like, when I was ten. I wasn't interested in girls. Only the bad, rash, adventuresome boys in my class. Most of whom were not my friends, which made things a little easier. I learned pretty quickly that liking the other guys more than girls was something to stay away from in this crowd of boys.

I'd kept that secrecy, that quiet sense of shame, of being in the wrong, my whole life. I had a feeling that while he hadn't articulated it—because he was trying to get the hell out and not be blamed for it—this was part of the reason that Graham had left. He knew, or sensed, that I wasn't capable of being open. Not that he helped.

It felt really good to be able to be honest—and angry—about Graham. I'd not run into him again after I saw him at the gym. I was grateful. While I'd calmed down, I was still angry at him. I didn't know how to let it go, and I was trying. But I thought about what he did, the bullshit that he laid at my door, rather than accepting the crap he'd done, and it pissed me off all over again. I'd been ignoring it because I didn't want to have that anger impede on my time with Declan in any fashion, but with him being gone, it was me and my thoughts.

Which left a lot of time for thought. Probably too much thought. Over thinking things was usually not a good thing.

No, I came to the conclusion that I would need to see Graham and speak my piece. Let him know that I knew, that I knew who and what he was, and tell him I was angry.

And then I would tell him I never wanted to see him again. It would be done. I would be done, and that chapter of my life would be over. A memory.

For the first time since we'd broken up, I was ready to let him go.

I just didn't realize how quickly I'd get my chance.

19

*D*eclan was still stuck at his parents. He said it would probably be another week, and I wasn't looking forward to the weekend alone. I sounded Tib out, but she and Seth were taking her boat out, and they'd be gone all weekend. No one saw X anymore. He was on a perpetual honeymoon.

So it was just me. I went for a run on Saturday morning, shopped, and did all the chore-like things I could think of.

I was missing Declan.

Midday, I thought, I'm doing the same damn thing I did with Graham. Making someone else my life. I adored the guy, but I don't want to be in the same shitty place a couple of years from now.

So I texted some of the guys from the basketball team and joined them out for a beer. I found that I had fun, and I laughed and drank more than I should have.

When I got home, after having to call Uber, I fell into bed. I needed to do that more often. I checked my phone again. Declan hadn't called.

This much silence felt… not right somehow. I texted him.

Hey, I miss you. I hope everything is as okay as it can be. I'm here if you need me.

Then I waited.

A watched pot never boils. Neither does a watched phone. He didn't text back.

Sunday morning, I got up and went for a run again, my frustration at missing Declan and not hearing from him resulting in a seven-mile run in which I did my best to wear myself out.

When I got home, I leaned against the tree in front of my place, stretching and working out my still-tense muscles. I felt someone come near me, and I moved over so that I wasn't blocking the sidewalk.

Looking up to see if I needed to move further, I saw Graham standing in front of me, hands in his pockets, looking like he'd lost his best friend.

"Hey," he said.

I noted that he didn't sound confident, smug, or gleeful, as he had the last time I'd seen him.

"What do you want?"

His eyes looked like they were tearing up. Really?

"I didn't expect that, Bry."

"Bryant."

"What?"

"Bry is my nickname, reserved for my friends. You aren't a friend anymore."

"You don't mean that."

How in the hell did he dredge up the nerve to look shocked?

"I do. What do you want?"

"Can I come in and talk to you?"

I sighed, letting the leg I'd been stretching drop. "What else is there to say?"

"More than I want to be saying in the middle of a side-walk!" Some of his old Graham attitude surfaced.

I sighed again. I really didn't want to talk to him, for all my big promises to myself. It felt wearisome, and tedious. Be careful what you wish for, right? It was hard not to roll my eyes in front of him. I wondered if Dhameer had made this happen—which was surprising. I hadn't thought of him, or wishes, or anything like that in weeks.

That's when I knew I'd moved on completely. It wasn't even worth it to yell at Graham. I just didn't care anymore.

But I also wasn't an asshole, and he looked all pitiful.

"Fine. You can have fifteen minutes, and then we're done."

"What, do you have a hot date?"

"No. I just don't want to hear any more." I didn't wait for his answer but moved to the front door. As I stepped in, I didn't turn to see if he followed me in.

He would. He obviously had something he needed to get off his chest. Fine. Let him say whatever, and then he could leave. And I could take a shower and think about Declan.

I went to the kitchen to get a glass of water. I didn't offer him any. I didn't want him to feel welcome, or to try to stay. When I'd drunk half the glass, I set it down on the counter, and then looked at the clock, and back to Graham.

"Your fifteen minutes start now. What is it?"

He shoved his hands in his pockets, a sure sign that he was nervous. I remembered that I hadn't seen it very often —he wasn't usually nervous with me.

With my new eyes, I wondered if that was because I took whatever shit he dished out. I was so in love with him.

And he didn't appreciate that. The way he left showed me that.

Perhaps the shoe was on the other foot? It was interesting to think about, but not right now. I needed to focus on hearing him out and then getting him to leave.

Even though a part of me was astounded. Two months ago, I'd have been delighted to have him standing here.

"I miss you," he said.

"Okay." I didn't say anything else.

He waited. I wondered what he was expecting. But then, I wasn't the same guy he left standing with a marriage proposal in hand. He didn't know that.

"I wanted to tell you that I am sorry about how things ended between us."

I blinked. Did he really just say that? "You're sorry? For how things ended?" I repeated slowly.

"Yes. I know that I—"

I held up a hand. "You cheated on me."

He opened his mouth, probably to deny it. I shook my head.

"No, don't bother with denials. I asked you to marry me, you said yes, and then when I hesitated on something, said, well fuck this, and hauled ass out of here. With your pre-packed bag," I narrowed my eyes. "To a car that was waiting for you. For the life of me, I'll never understand why you didn't just say no. But I've thought about it—I don't think you expected me to pop the question. I think you were on your way out, and I momentarily distracted you from your goal. It doesn't matter," I shook my head again. "I also know that you were cheating before you left."

He was surprised, but then his normal, confident air took over. "Now you're just talking crazy. Does that make you feel better?"

"No, it made me feel worse. But I know you went

straight to someone else's house, and then later information revealed you'd been a couple with this guy before we ended." I shrugged. "Seems pretty simple to me. You met someone else and didn't want to tell me."

I crossed my arms, leaning against the counter in the kitchen. Light came in through the window, putting him in a spotlight. The light made him look like a painting.

But it was a painting I was no longer a fan of.

"Which is fine. Things change, people fall out of love. But you could have told me, you could have said no to my proposal. Instead, you led me on, told me it was my fault we couldn't get married. And for what? To ease your shitty guilt? That's what pisses me off, Graham! I have no problem with unpleasant truth! But you didn't give me that! You pawned your bullshit off on me, and made me question myself, made me wonder why I wasn't enough, what I did wrong." I stopped, looking up at the ceiling and taking a breath.

Then I looked at him again. "When in truth, the problem was you. You were cheating, fucking some other guy while still professing to love me. Had you been honest, this could have been avoided. But you would have had to take responsibility for your actions, and there seems to be a lot of an avoidance of that, doesn't there?"

He looked at me, and I could tell he was trying to find the words to refute what I said.

He couldn't. His head dropped. Then he met my eyes again. "Yes. You're right. All of it. I'm a shit, and I treated you like shit. But you're wrong. I have always loved you. Always. I was angry because you wouldn't be honest about me, about us. About what we were together. Your family thought I was just your good friend, your roommate," he sneered the word. "And you did nothing to change that. You let them think less of me."

I interrupted then. "They didn't think less of you. They knew you were one of my best friends, and they valued you for that. There was no lessening of you, or what you were to me. You were important in my life, and they knew that. Don't distract. You want me to believe that you cheated because my family didn't know about us?"

"Yes! You were totally fine with them thinking one thing about us, which wasn't true! How do you think that feels? My family knew about us! They knew we lived together as a couple, not roommates! I was honest with them! You never gave me that same courtesy."

"You're right. I didn't. And for that, I'm sorry. It must have hurt. But that doesn't mean you get a pass on your hurting me. You mind fucked me, Graham. You know you did. I get that you were angry, and from a distant perspective, I understand. But for me, up close, no, I don't understand. You made something that wasn't ideal utter shit. To avoid the fact that you cheated." I shrugged again. "Listen, I thought I wanted to see you, tell you all about yourself, and now that you're here, I find I don't want to rehash everything."

"Why? You're so happy with your new lover boy?"

"What I am doing or who I'm with is not your concern. Why did you want to see me?" I wasn't going to entertain any discussion on Declan. It occurred to me that Graham was fishing. He didn't know that Declan and I were together. Well, he wouldn't know. He'd have to wonder.

Graham squared his shoulders. "It doesn't seem like I've done a good job getting to that, but I wanted to ask you if we could try again."

"I'm sorry, what?" I must have heard wrong.

"I want to try again. I want to come back."

"Come back how?"

"Let me come home," he said. His eyes were soft, and he had a small smile on his face.

"Move back in?"

"Yes, to start. Maybe not in the same room," he added. "So that we can work on things."

"We don't need to work on a thing," I turned around and faced the sink, looking out the window. "There is no we, Graham."

I heard him come up behind me, and then his arms went around my waist. He kissed the spot between my shoulder blades that used to make me shiver. "Yes, there is. Listen to us. We're finally having the fight that we needed to. This is a good thing, Bryant," he said, resting his head in the spot he'd just kissed.

My focus was so centered on Graham and managing my own emotions that I didn't hear anything else.

Until I heard a voice said, "Well, this is interesting. Am I interrupting?"

I nearly strained my head whipping my head around. Declan stood in the hallway at the entrance to the kitchen, a bag on his shoulder and another one in his hand. I'd forgotten that I'd given him a key. Just in case. Figures that it was now that he decided to use it.

"I didn't know you were coming back today," I said. Fuck. That sounded guilty as hell.

"Clearly. I can come back later if that's—"

"That would be good," Graham said. He'd turned and had an arm around my waist. Like we were a couple or something.

"No, that wouldn't be good. Graham was just leaving." I removed his arm, glaring at him.

"Was I?"

"Yes. Everything that needed to be said has been said."

His eyes searched my face. "Are you sure, Bry?"

He did that deliberately. What a shit.

"Yes, Graham, we don't have anything more to say. It's time for you to leave."

We stared at one another. In the past, I had a hard time maintaining my position with him. It was all part of the shit I was wrapped up in, all the guilt, and the worry, and my entire life. I felt guilty for being gay, and then guilty for not being open about who I was, and guilty for subjecting someone else to it —the past months with Declan had forced me to see that.

And it was all wrapped up in how I let things go on between Graham and me.

But no more.

"I can see you have some things you need to sort out," he gave Declan an up-and-down glance. "We can continue this conversation later."

"Oh for fuck's sake," I said, my patience gone. "There's nothing left for us to discuss. Please don't come by again. We're done. You know the way out," I said.

"I should. I lived here," he snapped back, and walked out of the kitchen past Declan. A moment later, I heard the front door close.

I met Declan's eyes. There was a decidedly neutral expression on his face.

"I'm sorry," I said. "No one should have to see that."

"Was he always like that?"

I went to the table and sat down. Dealing with Graham made me tired all of a sudden. "I want to say no, because I never saw it. But I think he was." I gave him a half-smile. "I just didn't see it."

He set down his bags and came over to me, putting his arms around me. "We all have relationships that we realize weren't a good idea."

"Yeah, but is yours going to march up to your house and stir shit?"

He sighed. "You never know."

"How's your dad?" I turned around to give him a one-armed hug. "I didn't think you were coming home this week."

"I had to come back for some work stuff. So I told my mom I'd fly back Wednesday night. It's been hard. I feel like we're on a death watch, and I'm the only one. My mom knows, I think."

"Is your dad awake?"

He rested his head on my shoulder, and I could feel the weariness on him. "Sometimes. He falls asleep a lot, like in mid-sentence. And I don't think he's all there when he is awake."

"I'm sorry," I said again.

"There's nothing you or me or anyone else can do. I just have to get through it. I'm supposed to meet with his attorney when I get back. That will be fun," he sighed. He stood up and pulled me up from the chair. "But enough of that. Let's say hello the right way."

He wrapped his arms around me and kissed me. I kissed him back, letting all the things I'd been feeling since he'd left, and all the awareness that had come to me flow into it. I wanted him to know how much I felt for him.

It was like kissing a dream.

"You are so damn sexy, but I'm about to fall down. Will you boot me if I say I'd love to take a shower, and then just lay down with you?"

What I wanted was to strip him naked and stay up all night, but I could hear how tired he was. "I won't boot you, but I will need a moment to manage my raging attraction to you," I said, pulling him closer. You know, just so he could be assured of said raging attraction.

"What if I promise to make it up to you?"

"Then," I said, kissing him once more, "You have a deal. My shower is yours."

He held me and I felt something new, and wonderful, pass between us.

As he let go of me and picked up his bag, heading for my bathroom, I watched him.

Was this love?

he question floored me. Was it? I'd fallen in love with Graham over time. There was a lot of flirting, of back and forth. It had taken a while for us to finally tell one another how we felt. Looking back, it was one more way that he played the control in our relationship.

That made me sad to think the most significant love relationship I'd ever had was nothing that I'd thought it was.

However, it led me to Declan. Or rather, to be able to appreciate Declan. So perhaps all the bullshit was worth it.

I was so happy that he didn't go all ape shit and start a huge fight about Graham being here. I was expecting all kinds of drama, but there was none. He asked what happened, I told him, and he believed me. This was how things were supposed to be. I went upstairs and laid in my bed, waiting for him to shower. As I listened to the water in the other room, another sound came through.

It sounded like… I sat up. Got up quietly and went to the bathroom door.

Declan was crying.

My heart nearly broke listening to him. I walked back to the bed and laid down. All I wanted to do was rush in and comfort him, but there was something to be said for being able to grieve privately. I wasn't going to take that away from him.

He came out about ten minutes later. The steam rose off him as he dried his hair with a towel. He looked good enough to... well, do a lot of things to.

Easy, I told myself. Don't be that guy.

"Can I stay with you tonight?" He asked.

"Like you even have to ask."

The small smile that elicited pushed me further into the broken heart category.

"Come here with me." I held out an arm.

"I'll be there in a minute." He went back into the bathroom. When he came out, he was wearing boxers, and he crawled into bed with me, resting his head on my shoulder.

When we'd met, I'd needed the shoulder. It felt good to be someone who another person would lean on. To be the shoulder.

"You want to talk?" I asked.

"No, if that's all right," Declan said.

"No worries," I said. "I'm just trying to make you comfortable."

"I missed this. I missed you," he said.

"I missed you, too."

Declan didn't speak again. I could hear his breathing relax, and as I listened to it, I fell asleep with him.

"Sasha!"

I woke up, heart racing. Declan was sitting up in bed next to me, his eyes wide.

"Sasha!" He said again.

"Declan, are you okay?" I put a hand on his arm.

He jumped as though he'd been shot.

"What… where am I?" He turned wide eyes to me.

"It's me, Declan. Bryant. Everything's okay."

"As long as she's safe," he said. He lay back down, and within a few moments, was asleep again.

What in the name of hell had that been about? It took me a long time to fall back to sleep.

---

*T*he next morning, when I woke, Declan was gone. I got up to see if he'd just gotten up before me. But his bags were gone. I looked around, and he hadn't left a note.

If he hadn't woken up in a cold fear the night before, I wouldn't feel a thread of unease, but since he had, I did.

I sighed. No use in making something more than it was. I got ready for work and headed in early.

Mid-afternoon, Declan called.

"Hey," I said. "How are you?"

"Up to my ass," he said. "Sorry I left so early. I couldn't sleep."

I waited to see if he'd mention the fact he'd woken up in the middle of the night, but he didn't.

"You want to get together tonight?"

He sighed. "I do, but I'm not sure when I'll be done. How about tomorrow?"

I was disappointed, but I understood. "Sure. Come over for dinner."

"I'd like that," his voice was warm, and it was the Declan I knew.

"All right. Just text when you're on your way." I didn't

really want to leave things until I saw him tomorrow, but I also didn't want to be the clingy boyfriend, all about me when he had a lot on his plate.

Declan surprised me the next night, because he got out of work before I did, and we spent a great evening together.

I told him about going out with the basketball guys, and he laughed. "I'm proud of you, Bry! I know that's not your comfort zone."

I laughed with him. "No, it's not, but I decided that I didn't want to just sit home."

"Good. You need to get out more."

"I agree." I kissed him. "Thanks for making me join you."

"It is my pleasure. Even though it's part of my grand plan to lure you in," he said, kissing my ear.

"It's working."

"Is it?" He murmured. "How about you show much just how well it's working?"

"Why don't you follow me?" I said. I stood, pulling his hand.

"I could almost think you planned this," he said, grinning.

"Yeah, like twelve seconds ago. But it's a good plan, isn't it?"

We made love all night long. I'd never laughed so much with another person, not even Tib. His intensity made me gasp, and the tender way he looked at me was something I'd never thought I'd experience.

It was glorious.

I had a sneaking feeling that yes, in fact this was very much love.

The next morning, we lingered over saying goodbye.

"I have to catch my flight right after work," he said in

between kisses.

"When do you think you'll be back?" I asked.

"It depends."

I knew what that meant.

"I hope everything goes well, I mean, as well as it can," I amended.

"Thanks, Bry. And thanks for being here for me. It means more than you know."

"I'm here," I said. "Take your time."

"Thank you," he kissed me again, and I felt my knees melt, my entire being dissolve at his touch.

Even the simple act of a kiss had become glorious.

Yeah, it was love.

---

*T*hree more days passed. I played basketball on Wednesday and made plans to join them for beers again on Saturday. But first, I had to go to brunch with Tibby and Seth, and caught them up on all the doings in my life. Not that I minded. Tibby was a constant in my life and I'd been neglecting her outside of work.

"I cannot believe that Graham just showed up. What an asshole. He's totally like herpes," Tibby said.

"Yeah, he tried to play it off on the whole cheating thing."

"Well, you know the truth. And fuck him. How's Declan?"

"I haven't talked to him much. I get the impression his mom is as tough as his dad, for different reasons."

"Where's he from?" Seth asked.

"Indiana," I said. "Kokomo, actually."

"Did you sing the song when you heard that?" Tibby asked.

Seth and I looked at her.

"What? It's the first thing that came to my head. Your parents didn't listen to the Beach Boys?"

Both of us shook our heads.

"Explains a lot," she said, taking a drink of her coffee.

"Okay, whatever, weirdo," I said. "It sounds like there's a lot going on that he hasn't told me, but even though I want to know, I get it. No one wants to spill all their family shit."

"I totally get that," Tibby said.

"Well, you do have an interesting family," Seth said.

"Look, your family is practically a fifties sitcom," Tibby said. "I didn't grow up like that. I didn't want you to meet them and think this was your future. So I get why people might keep some family dirt to themselves."

"It makes sense. I just wish things didn't feel out of whack."

"What do you mean?" Tibby asked.

"Ever since he came in and found Graham in my place, it's felt like there's a distance between us."

"I can't imagine he's worried about Graham," Tibby said immediately.

Seth looked at her, smiling. "And why is that, oh guru?"

"Have you seen Declan? I mean, we did meet the same guy, right?" She shook her head. "Holy shit. That guy is beautiful. Graham's good looking, but next to Declan? No comparison. Declan is a thing of beauty. And Graham's a shitty person."

"A thing of beauty?" Seth asked. "I'm right here."

"Whatever," she waved a hand at him.

"He is a thing of beauty," I said to Seth. "I have to agree with her."

"You're not supposed to take her side anymore," Seth complained. "It's you and me against the machine, man!"

We all laughed.

Tibby said, "It's fine, Bry. His dad is dying. Sounds like his mom isn't accepting it. And who knows what else is going on? Just try to relax. You've been doing such a good job up until now. Don't backslide!"

It felt good to just hang out with them. I felt better, too, about my worries. Tib was right. I couldn't ask a lot when he was up to his eyeballs in family stuff.

My feeling of well-being continued when I met the guys Saturday night. They asked about Declan, and I told them a little, and then we moved on.

I got up Sunday and went running. It had been a great week. I felt badly that Declan was dealing with so much sadness, and I decided that I'd call him when I got back.

But I got distracted, and made myself a late breakfast, and then cleaned up. All the chores I'd been ignoring for the last week demanded attention as well. By the time I looked at the clock, it was after one.

I wanted to call him before it got too late. Maybe he'd be at lunch, where he could talk. There were no cells allowed on the floor where his dad was staying.

Grabbing my phone, I settled into the couch, and then called him. For fun, I hit the 'video' button. I really wanted to see him.

When he picked up, he hit the video option as well, and he was walking.

"Hey, you," I said. "I hope I'm not interrupting."

"No, I'm having lunch with... with family," he said. He glanced over his shoulder as he walked into a room and closed the door.

"Oh, well I won't keep you then," I said, feeling guilty.

"No, it's good to see you," he said, and while there was something on his face that I couldn't interpret, he did look glad to see me.

"How's your dad?"

He sighed. "It's only a matter of time. Like, a few days at the most. My mom is still there, but I had to leave for a couple of things today, so we're—I'm having some lunch before… I go back."

"I am so sorry."

He shrugged. "I feel bad for my mom. This is going to be really hard on her. I think she's finally accepting it, but not gracefully."

"How'd the talk with the lawyer go?" I asked.

Whatever he was going to say was lost as the door behind him burst open.

A little girl with dark hair in pigtails flew in.

A dark-haired woman was right behind her.

"I'm sorry," she said to Declan. "She got away from me. Come on, honey, let's leave Daddy alone."

The little girl tried to wriggle away from the woman's arms, and the woman said, "Sasha! Daddy's working. Come on." She shot Declan, and me, an apologetic look. *Sorry*, she mouthed. She hurried back out, shutting the door behind her.

Declan turned back to the phone and there was fear on his face. "Bryant…"

"Daddy?" I asked.

He sighed, defeat and ten years settling across his face. "Yes. She—"

I held up a hand. "I don't want to hear it, Declan. Not right now. I need to go."

"No, Bryant, let me explain!"

"No."

I clicked the red button, ending the call. I put my phone on mute and then went and laid down in bed.

How in the fuck had this happened again? What was wrong with me?

21

The sun went behind the clouds in the window. I'd been lying in bed since the call with Declan. I assumed he called, but since I'd left my phone on mute, and not looked at it once—a testament to my willpower, or my despair, I wasn't sure which—I had no idea.

Daddy.

The little girl—Sasha—had called him daddy.

And who was the woman? Presumably his wife. He was married.

Married would have been bad enough, but he was married to a woman.

And all that talk about honesty.

What the fuck? What the actual fuck?

I didn't know what to think. Except that I'd fallen for a bunch of shit *again*. It pissed me off to no end.

Just when I'd admitted to myself that I'd fallen in love. And that hurt. I could feel a couple of tears leak out of the corner of my eyes, but more than anything, I was pissed.

Even though part of me was seething with anger at

being lied to again, the other part of me was just worn out. I didn't want to move from where I was.

So I went to sleep.

Maybe this would all be better in the morning.

I rolled over and willed myself to sleep. If I slept, I didn't have to think, or feel.

Which was fine with me.

The next morning, I called Tibby early, before she left for work.

"I'm not coming in today," I said.

"What's wrong?" She asked.

"Worst day I've had in a long time," I said. "I'm a damn mess, and I need a sick day."

"Well, you never take any, so have at it."

Tibby was a good friend—she knew to leave me be. I'd tell her eventually, but I couldn't tell her now. I just couldn't.

"Thanks, Tib. I'm sorry for the last minute—"

"Stop right there. It's fine. We'll be fine. You take whatever time you need, and I'll be here if you need anything."

"Thanks." I said.

About two hours after I talked to her, the doorbell rang. I shuffled down the stairs, and there was a delivery guy.

"Bryant Higgs?"

"Yes."

"Here you go," he said, handing me a box that was warm. "Have a great day!"

I went back to the kitchen and opened the box.

Strawberries and cream pancakes from Uprising Muffins. I smiled. This was all Tibby. It was one of our favorite breakfast places.

Food held no interest for me until right this moment, smelling those pancakes. I sat down and ate every bit.

I texted her after I finished.

You are the best friend evah. Love you.

Love you too. Call me when you're ready. She responded immediately.

I didn't text back. Tibby understood.

Then I went back to bed.

---

*T*wo days later, I was tired of myself. Yes, this sucked. Yes, it hurt like a bitch. Yes, I was mad at myself.

But none of that would do me any good. It was Wednesday, and I wanted to go to the games tonight. I did not, however, want to run into Declan.

He'd been calling and texting since Sunday. The one today said:

My dad is gone. I'm wrapping up here and I'll be home by next week. Please say you'll see me.

I didn't respond. Just like I hadn't to any of his earlier messages. I wasn't ready to speak to him. However, that meant I'd probably be able to get out and play some basketball tonight without my abject relationship failure staring me in the face.

"How the fuck is this getting me anywhere in my wish, Dhameer?" I asked out loud. I'd forgotten that this whole damn mess started because a djinn said I had to change and improve my life, or some shit, and then I'd get my heart's desire. My fixation on that faded once I realized that Graham wasn't my happily ever after.

And frankly, I'd been so happy spending time with

Declan, I hadn't even thought of it since the beginning of our relationship.

But I thought of it now.

"What the hell? What is this teaching me, exactly?" I remembered that Tib said she'd had to learn and grow. "I'm growing, all right. Pissed and bitter. That's how I'm growing."

The silent house offered me no answer.

"Fuck this," I said, and got up. I was going to shower, take off the clothes I'd been wearing for the past however many days, and go back to life.

Without a djinn, or Declan, or any of the shit that was dragging me down.

"It's taught you to be honest, has it not?"

I whipped around to see the djinn in all his sparkly glory, hovering in my kitchen.

"Yeah, and what a price I've paid! It's one fucking mess after the other! You said, if I change, I'll get my heart's desire! I've done all kinds of changing, and what do I meet? Some guy who's married! To a woman! With a kid!"

Dhameer had his arms crossed, and he merely watched as I worked myself up into a complete fit.

"Isn't there some kind of limit on how much hard knocks learning someone has to do at once? Because I could do without this! Not to mention that some kind of warning would have been nice."

"There are no warnings from on high somewhere in life," his voice was calm. "You have to develop your own warnings. Listening to your inner voice—"

"My inner voice! Oh, now I have to find that, too? This is bullshit!"

I threw my hands up and stomped up the stairs. "Keep your damn wish! I'm doing just fine with falling into shit all by myself. I don't need your kind of help!"

There was no answer.

Dhameer was really unsatisfying in a fight. Damn the man. Djinn. Whatever. I showered and headed out.

I was a little late, so I didn't have time to answer any awkward questions about Declan. I was glad because at the moment I couldn't say anything good.

Nor did I want to out him as leading a double life. Mad as I was, it wasn't my place.

"Shit, man, what's up with you? You're on fire tonight," Steve said.

"Rough week at work. Can't punch clients," I lied.

He laughed. "And people always think the lawyer has the short end of the stick."

"Sometimes, but not this week," I forced a laugh.

"I wouldn't go up against you," he said.

By the time we finished, I didn't feel like there was a bubble of rage that was just waiting for the right moment to burst. I was able to go home and get the first good night of sleep since I'd heard Sasha call Declan 'Daddy'.

I reminded myself to work out more often. Running was good, but there was something satisfying about playing like this on a team.

No matter what happened with Declan and me, I wasn't going to hibernate. I wasn't going to drop this league thing, and I wasn't going to sulk one God-damned moment longer.

I had a smile on my face as I fell asleep.

I went into work on Thursday and Friday. Tibby asked me if I wanted to talk, and I told her that I wasn't ready. I'd decided that I wasn't going to give up on anything, but that didn't mean I needed to pick at the wound.

So when the weekend rolled around, I felt like I could handle it. I wouldn't be fantastic, but I wouldn't be a complete mess, either.

I'd ordered Chinese from my favorite place and cued up a couple of movies on Netflix.

While I was waiting, Xavier called.

"Hey man, what's up?"

"Aren't you supposed to be living on a cloud of love or something? You back already?"

"Yeah, we just got back, and—"

"You talked to Tib."

"Course I did. You should too. What's going on?"

"Life sucks ass right now."

I could almost see X's shrug. "It does indeed sometimes. Did I hear Tib right? Did you meet Dhameer?"

I rolled my eyes. "Yes, and he's an unhelpful pain in my ass. I hope you heard that!" I yelled at the room.

Xavier burst out laughing. "If I wasn't sure that you'd met him that would give it away. Once I'd remembered that I'd met him, I yelled at my empty place, too. The glitter never stopped, man. It was like he dumped buckets of the shit."

"A little help would be nice. I haven't seen that much glitter, myself." I knew I sounded like a little kid who lost his favorite toy. Although in my defense, I'd lost a hell of a lot more than that. I also admitted to myself that I would have appreciated more glitter. It would mean Dhameer was around, trying to help me.

"According my beloved, you can only help yourself. We never listen to people who are trying to help us."

"Maybe you don't," I grumbled.

"No, I sure as hell don't. But listen, I didn't call to talk about genie smart asses. I wanted to know if you wanted to come up, now that Liv and I are back in the real world."

"I don't know," I said, a grin coming over my face. "Are you guys fit for the real world? You were pretty unfit the last time I saw you."

"Don't be hatin'," X said mildly. "Not everyone can have my outstanding skills."

I heard Olivia burst into laughter in the background.

"Listen, man, I'm serious. Anything you need, I'm here."

"I appreciate it. But I'm good."

"Well, that's the thing. Tib says otherwise."

I sighed. "She's right, but there's nothing I can do but get through it. If I just can't stand myself anymore, I'll come up and see you. Good enough?"

"Yeah. I'll hold you to it. You get another month, at the most."

He hung up. He wasn't big on goodbyes.

Another month? I wouldn't make it going on like this. I'd managed to put a Band-Aid on my hurts, but I knew that it was only temporary. I had to find a way to let go of my anger and move on.

Which sounded perfectly shitty. Not to mention, a shit ton of work I didn't want to do.

Fuck it, I thought. No deep shit tonight. Tonight it was Chinese and Netflix.

When I got up Saturday, I could tell that I'd eaten too much Chinese. Even though they didn't use MSG, I could always feel my fingers swell. I drank a huge glass of water and went for a run.

As I returned home, I could see there was someone sitting on my steps. I slowed, wanting to get a look—it was Declan.

He stood when he saw me and held out his hands. "Bryant, can we please talk?"

I shrugged. "What is there to talk about? You have a

daughter. I'm guessing you're married. I'm not sure how you square that with living out here, but I don't care. I don't have time or energy for people who lie to me. You know, the people who aren't honest?" I stressed the last word.

It was funny how in the last month, both the men I'd fallen for had shown up at my door, wanting to talk. Since I was the common denominator, I thought maybe I needed to look at me. Damn. Maybe I would need to talk to a therapist, or something. See what my asshole magnet was all about.

He winced. "Yes. You're right. I wasn't honest, but—"

"No. Don't give me a yes, and then follow that with an excuse. Because that's all it is. An excuse."

"Then will you let me explain it to you? No excuses?"

I stared at him, wanting to stay angry. Then I sighed. "All right. Come in."

He followed me in, and unlike when I had to do this before with Graham, I was a little nicer. "I'm going to grab some water, and then you can explain. You want some?"

"Yes, please." He stopped, waiting in the living room.

I hurried to get a couple of glasses and told my heart to stop. I didn't need it beating out of my chest.

Somehow, I didn't want to hear what he had to say. It was going to make the hurt worse.

But that's not how you managed. You heard the truth, and you handled it, and you moved forward. Learning to be honest meant you took the good with the bad. My ability to be honest was hard won, and I wasn't going to give it up, even if the next half-hour or whatever hurt like hell. I took a breath, steeled myself, and went back in to the living room.

Declan was still standing where he'd stopped, staring at the fireplace.

"Here," I said. "Sit down. Say what you need to say."

He took the glass and sat down across from me. Not meeting my eyes, he took a long drink.

The silence stretched on.

I wasn't going to break it. This wasn't my story, nor was it my burden. I didn't need to apologize or make excuses. So I stayed silent. I was proud of myself.

"I don't even know where to start," he said. "I've been thinking about how I wanted to tell you this, where the right place to begin was... and I've been going around in circles all week. I guess it starts in high school. You know what that's like," he looked at me then. "I didn't tell anyone I was gay. I had a girlfriend. I was on the football team. In Indiana. There wasn't any other way for me." He sighed.

"Then I went to college, to Ohio State."

"I thought your sisters confronted you in college," I said, doing my level best to keep my voice neutral.

"They did. I denied it, vehemently. I'll never forget how Addie, my oldest sister, looked at me. Like she knew I was lying. But I wasn't ready. I couldn't tell the truth." He sighed, looking down.

Then he looked back up at me. "So, I still kept up the pretense. But I knew, and it was like I was dying inside. I think you know what that's like, although I felt like the pressure was extreme. I played football my first two years, and there was no way in hell I could come out then. I wouldn't have made it out of the locker room alive.

"My junior year, I got cut. I was fine with it because I was tired of getting my ass handed to me. I wasn't bad, but I'm not a beast, and they don't fuck around. I met Mariana, and we started dating. We dated the rest of college, and she was... well, I could be okay with her. I wasn't myself, I didn't want to be in a straight relationship, but she was nice. She was—is—a good person. I'm no different from anyone else. I took what seemed the best, and easiest path at the time. We got married two years after we graduated, and Sasha came a year after that."

"Why didn't you tell me you had a daughter?" I asked.

"Because I would have to tell you all of this, and I wasn't ready to. You have to understand something. Moving here has allowed me, for the first time in my entire life, to be exactly who I want to be. Who I am," he added fiercely.

"You didn't even try. That's the complete opposite of honesty, and that's your thing, remember?" I said.

"I know. I *know*," he said again. "I felt like such a hypocrite! I've been kicking my own ass for days, weeks. I wanted to tell you—"

"But you didn't."

"No, I didn't." He sighed. "Mari and I are separated. We have been for the past four years. Sasha is five so that gives you an idea of how long my marriage has been over."

"Why aren't you divorced?"

"Insurance."

"What?"

"My father wasn't the only sick one," he said, his head falling. His voice broke. "Sasha was diagnosed with leukemia when she was two. Acute lymphocytic leukemia. She's in remission right now, but it can come back at any time. I had to stay there, we had to look married. Otherwise, Sasha wouldn't have had insurance. My little girl wouldn't have lived," he looked up, and there were tears in his eyes. "Once it was possible to get insurance with pre-existing conditions, I took a better job, and I moved away. Mari and I were already living separate lives. My mom knows, but she doesn't want to accept it. My dad—well, we told him we were working things out. He was so angry at me for leaving Sasha. Both Mari and I tried to tell him that we needed more—but he told me I was a coward, and a shit father, and he threw me out of his house."

Declan leaned back, sighing. "Mari is the one person who is not at fault here. She asked me point blank if I was gay when we split. I was so surprised. I didn't do anything, didn't have a secret boyfriend, nothing. She just said she knew. And she freed me. She told me to go. We've kept up the pretense for my family, and hers. But with my father passing—"

"I'm sorry, by the way," I said, feeling like shit. "I'm so sorry I didn't say anything—"

Declan waved his hand. "It's all right. This is my shit to manage. But thank you. I feel horrible, Bryant. I wanted to tell you, but I couldn't. It was—it just seemed like such a mess. I didn't want to drag you into it. That's why I completely understand how it feels to be free. For the first time in my life. Until I came here, right before I met you, I'd never been free. And you are the first person I've been with that has been completely, one-hundred percent my choice. Mine. Not because I was expected to be with someone, or felt I had to—I was with you because I wanted to be. Not to hide anything, or for any other reason than I— than you make me happy," he amended.

Holy.

Shit.

What do you say to that? I didn't even know where to start.

"How is Sasha?"

"She's okay, but she's been showing the symptoms of it again, the things we noticed right before she was diagnosed."

"Did you see her a lot before you moved out here?"

He nodded. "Every day. I miss her, I miss her like you

wouldn't believe. With my dad, and her not doing well, it was so hard to be there, knowing I was leaving. And knowing that I hadn't told you—"

"I wish you had," I said. His pain, his honesty—and I was pretty sure this was as honest as it got—made me feel humble, and ashamed. Yes, I'd been hurt, and had pain. But it was nothing like this.

"This is my shit," he said.

"When you're with someone, you share the burden." I said.

With those words, just like that, I forgave him. I knew. I knew what it felt like to have to hide, to feel you had no choice. Hadn't my last relationship blown up because of all my ideas of what was expected? Hadn't my whole life been a tale of caution, of being so careful, so that I wasn't exposed, or found out?

All because I thought who I was, the person I was, somehow was wrong. So had Declan. I got up, and went over to him, taking him in my arms. He reached up, putting a hand on my face.

"I can't believe you're not tossing me out on my ass," he said.

"How can I? I did the same thing you did, but you met me after all my shit blew up in my face."

"So… what's next?"

I shrugged. "How about you let me fix you something, and then after that… we'll see?"

The hope that I saw in his face still held fear. "Bryant, now that you know, I can't lie. I can't go that long without seeing my little girl again. I have to be there. If it's back—" he choked, his head dropping. Then he looked back up. "I can't leave her—or Mari—to handle this on their own. I won't. I know that's a lot to ask, but I can't lie anymore."

"I know. I wouldn't expect anything else."

"Have you gone through cancer with someone? It's the worse fucking thing you've ever done. I won't be a good boyfriend sometimes," he said.

"I'm not a good boyfriend sometimes. It's life. Now come on. Let's go see what there is to eat."

We walked with our arms around one another's waists into the kitchen, and I couldn't believe how at peace I felt. This wouldn't be easy. I would struggle with trust, and he would struggle with being a parent with one person, and a partner with the other.

But we would do this, and we'd do it together.

22

That night, as Declan slept, I got up. I couldn't fall asleep, so rather than toss and turn, and wake up someone who really needed to sleep, I headed down to the kitchen to make some tea. Maybe that would help me settle.

I'd been thinking about how to manage this new thing I'd fallen into ever since he told me. Once he'd come clean, Declan was wiped out. We hadn't talked much, and he fell asleep early.

There had to be something I could do to help him, to help this little girl. My family could—would—help. I knew they would. I just had to ask. I had to ask for help, which I never did.

Because it meant that I opened myself up to exposure.

Be open and welcoming, Dhameer had said. *Then you will get your wish—and the love, acceptance, and freedom you desire.*

I'd forgotten about all of that other than making changes and getting what I wanted. I had to be open. Accepting.

Like I'd done with Declan earlier today.

And I'd accept his life, and all the things that were in it, and we'd make it work. I felt more certain about this than I'd felt about anything in a long time.

"Very good," a deep voice said behind me.

I whipped around. Dhameer floated in the dark. I could see the sparkles from the ever-present glitter in the light from the lone lamp I'd turned on. The glitter made me think of Xavier's complaint, and I hid a grin and kept to the matter at hand.

"What do you mean?"

"You finally remembered all the terms of the wish you made, of our agreement. You needed to be open, and welcome others. You have finally done that. Now, you will get what it is you seek."

"This is it? This is for real?" Hope flared in my chest.

He nodded. "I wasn't sure you would succeed, Bryant Higgs. But you have. And I am pleased for you. I am pleased that you have made it through this set of challenges."

"Whoa, what do you mean, this set of challenges?"

He grinned, and it transformed his entire face. "Life is challenge, every single day. Haven't you learned that? It will be a challenge for the rest of your life. However, you are now equipped for it in a manner you have never been before."

I felt like he had conferred an honor on me, but I wasn't sure what it was.

"Thanks for not giving up on me," I said.

"I have found that I wanted all three of you to succeed," he said. "Your friend Tabitha is a truly good person, and she has chosen her friends wisely. So I wanted you to be happy. But you and Xavier—you have been a challenge. Even with that, I was interested in your success, and before you achieved it, I was hoping you would reach it. Even though…" He stopped.

"Sorry?" I said. I wasn't sure what he wanted to hear, and his words were all over the place.

"It is nothing. You are human, and challenge is part of who you are. But now, Bryant, I must go. Like you, I have completed a goal that was set for me, and my time with you is now up."

He smiled and I could sense the joy, the happiness from him. That was… weird. But whatever.

"Well, thank you. And good luck," I added, although I couldn't say why. It felt appropriate.

Dhameer bowed his head formally. "I thank you, Bryant Higgs. You are most welcome. If I may, I will leave you with one last piece of advice—when in doubt, always take the road of love." And with that, he disappeared.

The glitter, however, remained. I smiled, thinking about Xavier's complaints about the glitter. I hadn't noticed the copious amounts that he'd experienced. I'd have to mention that to him. Knowing Xavier, I rather thought he might have added to his glitter problem, but I couldn't be sure.

"Who were you talking to?" Declan was at the foot of the stairs.

I smiled again, loving the look of him sleepy. "You told me a pretty amazing story today. Now I have one to tell you. Just be open, okay?"

He made a face, but he sat down at the table. "Okay."

"So back in college, Tibby was having a bad night…"

EPILOGUE

One Year Later

I squeezed my mom's hand as I walked her in. My head whirled as I thought about what an amazing year this had been.

After I'd told Declan about Dhameer, and how he came into the lives of Tibby, X, and then me, he took a little while to believe it. But two weeks after that, we'd had lunch with Seth and Tibby and X and Olivia, and they backed me up. I think seeing that Seth and Olivia totally believed the whole thing helped to tip him into the 'I believe' camp.

I'd thought he was already there, but a couple of days after we'd seen my—now our—friends and their spouses, we were sitting out on the back deck.

"That's why," Declan said softly.

"What?" I asked, looking up from my laptop.

He looked over, and I realized that he hadn't been talking to me, not exactly.

"Do you remember the day we met?"

I nodded. "Of course. You threatened to have me sue myself," I smiled.

"Well, it was weird. I'd gone for a ride, but I didn't remember coming over to where your office was. I couldn't understand why I was there when that wasn't the route I'd planned."

"So?" I was missing something.

"Do you think your genie, or djinn, did it? Sent me that way, so we'd meet?"

I opened my mouth to say, no, of course not, when I stopped. Dhameer had told me that what I wished for would come once I'd started the work I needed to.

"I don't know," I said slowly. "Maybe."

"Well, good," Declan said. "I'm glad you did what you were supposed to."

I took his hand. "Me too."

It was one more thing that showed me that being honest was the best way.

In spite of how fabulous things were between us, I didn't ask him to move in with me. While I forgave him for lying to me, I decided that I needed to take time for myself, even as he and I were moving forward. We still didn't live together—well, not yet. I hadn't forgotten what I'd learned while I was working my way to getting my wish. In order to be someone else's forever, you had to make your own forever with yourself first.

Declan meeting my parents also happened shortly after we got back together. I wasn't going to make the same mistake twice. My parents really liked him — even my dad. I think it was playing Buckeye football that won my dad over.

That, and another grandchild.

They immediately adopted Sasha as though she were mine. When I told them about her, and Mari, and all that Declan and Mari had been doing for their daughter, my mom sprang into action.

Six months prior, Mari and Sasha had moved here. Sasha—she'd told me that I could call her Sashi—was still in remission, but it wasn't a sure thing. Thankfully, the hospitals here were amazing. Declan hadn't been sure that Mari would want to move, but it turned out that she was ready to move away, to get away from everything in Kokomo (no, we didn't sing the song, except for Tibby) and start over.

Coming here, with a support system in place, made it easier for Mari, and for Sasha. Between my mom and dad, they found her a job, and we helped her find a place to live. She and Sashi came to dinner with Declan and I a couple of times a week, and whenever we went to my big family dinners.

I didn't know what happened, but Melissa had come around. I was glad for Casey's sake. He loved his wife. He'd told me that it was as though someone flipped a switch. I resisted the urge to ask him if he'd noticed glitter in funny places at home. It didn't matter—I was delighted to see Casey Jr and Hannah again. I didn't think I'd ever have the relationship with Melissa I'd once had, but she was pleasant, and Sashi loved being around the kids. Melissa seemed to like Mari, which surprised me. Maybe that was it. I didn't know. But I didn't worry about it. It wasn't my concern.

The best part was that I'd never been happier. I loved Declan, and I'd told him shortly after we'd gotten back together. The amazing part, to me anyway, was that I didn't have any expectations of hearing it back, but he'd said, "I love you, too," with no hesitation.

I had a family. A family of my own. Me, Declan, Sashi, and Mari. It wasn't your typical family, but it was mine.

All because I'd finally let down my walls and come out of the closet in every way. I was open and welcoming. And now, the most darling girl in the world was walking towards me. She stepped carefully, aware of the importance of the event.

When she got close to me, I reached out a hand for her, which she took.

"How did I do, Brydad?" Sashi asked.

She'd started calling me Brydad, since she said she got to have another dad. I still couldn't hear it without getting choked up.

"You did great, sweets," I said. "Now let's watch for Daddy."

Declan came in, arm in arm with his mom. I didn't know what had happened there, either, but he and his mom had mended fences. He wore a tux, and he beamed at me. His mom looked more happy and relaxed than I'd ever seen her.

He finally got up to where I stood, hand in hand with his daughter, surrounded by the people who loved us. Xavier and Tibby stood next to me, and on the other side of Declan stood Mari. She held out a hand, and after Sashi handed me the rings, she hurried over to her mom.

"We ready?" Granddad boomed.

Declan and I turned to face him. I could feel the joy from Declan. It matched mine. I nodded at Granddad.

"Well, then, since the District of Columbia still allows me to do this, let's get this show on the road. Dearly beloved, we're gathered here to marry these two." He smiled at Declan and I.

I felt a sprinkle on my head, and I looked up. We were inside. There was no chance at rain.

Then I felt Declan pluck at the arm of my tux.

Glitter.

I looked up again and sent up a thank you. Words weren't enough, but they were all I had. I also sent my own wish to Dhameer, that he was happy, as happy as he'd made me, and Tib, and X.

"You with us, son?" Granddad asked.

"Yes," I said enthusiastically.

Granddad leaned forward, and in the worst stage whisper ever, said, "It's not quite time for that."

Declan and I looked at one another and smiled as the people with us laughed.

"So now that the grooms are paying attention, Bryant, you ready?"

I nodded, squeezing Declan's hand.

"All right. Here we go," Granddad said.

And the whole world opened up for us.

The End

AFTERWORD

I hope you've enjoyed the Djinn Everlasting series. I have so enjoyed writing it! And if you've been with me since Three Wishes, you know that Dhameer had a challenge before he ever met Tibby.

Click the link below, and you'll see how things end for him.

If you can't click, please visit https://dl.bookfunnel.com/1eva2rq2bo and you'll be able to access the post script story.

THE HEART OF THE DJINN

CLICK HERE TO DOWNLOAD

ACKNOWLEDGMENTS

How can I explain the excitement that comes from finishing a series? Particularly a series that is two years in the making? Three Wishes initially released in December 2015, and I've had the subsequence stories in my head ever since.

I have so many people that are part of this, so I apologize if I miss anyone!

Judy and Richard Crane, Shannon and Mike Scanlon, Linden and Liz Price, Corinne O'Flynn, Rachel Millar, and my darling husband and children. You all support me through all the stages of writing, and I do not have the words.

My tribe of writer friends. I wouldn't make it without you.

And my readers. You make every bit of this worthwhile.

ABOUT THE AUTHOR

Lisa Manifold is a USA Today Bestselling Author of fantasy, paranormal, and romance stories. She moved to Colorado as an adult and has no plans of living anywhere else. She is a consummate reader, often running late because "Just one more page!" Lisa writes the things she does because she really, really wants to live in a world where these kinds of stories happen.

She is a fan of all things Con, and has an entire room devoted to the costumes created for Cons. She served on the board of Rocky Mountain Fiction Writers for four years, and in 2016, was named the 2016-2017 RMFW Independent Writer of the Year.

Lisa is the author of the fae paranormal romance series The Realm, the Grimm fairy tale retelling Sisters of the Curse series, the Djinn Everlasting series which follows a free-lance djinn, the Aumahnee Prophecy urban fantasy series, and the forthcoming urban fantasy series The Dragon Thief.

She lives as close to the mountains as possible with her husband, sons, and three attentive dogs.

Connect with Lisa online:
www.lisamanifold.com
Lisa@lisamanifold.com

TITLES BY LISA MANIFOLD

The Realm Series

Heart of the Goblin King

To Wed the Goblin King

Realms of the Goblin King

Rise of the Dragon King

The Companion Tales, Volume I

The Companion Tales, Volume II (2018)

The Aumahnee Prophecy

with Corinne O'Flynn

Marigold's Tale (Prequel)

Eamonn's Tale (Prequel)

The Gim Crackers (Aumahnee World Novella)

The Portal Keepers (Aumahnee World Novella)

Watchers of the Veil

Djinn Everlasting

Three Wishes

Forgotten Wishes

Hidden Wishes

Sisters of the Curse

Thea's Tale

One Night at the Ball

Casimir's Journey

Do you like being in the loop? Sign up for Lisa's newsletter!
Shenanigans, book recs, and the latest news abound!